In the world of the light, where the angels ruled eternally, by the power of the invisible forces, two souls were gathered. With the love of their spirit, they had promised to each other once in the earth, they would wait for each other and when they would be ready for each other they would look for one another and gathered again once together they would proclaim the light of the angels with their peace kingdom melodies blowing the love of their minds.

AuthorHouse™ UK
1663 Liberty Drive
Bloomington, IN 47403 USA
www.authorhouse.co.uk
Phone: UK TFN: 0800 0148641 (Toll Free inside the UK)
UK Local: 02036 956322 (+44 20 3695 6322 from outside the UK)

Published by AuthorHouse 11/28/2020

ISBN: 978-1-6655-8258-2 (sc)
ISBN: 978-1-6655-8259-9 (hc)
ISBN: 978-1-6655-8257-5 (e)

authorHOUSE

CHAPTER 1
THE ENCHANTER'S YOUTH

There was once in the earth a shy child. He was born in an old and big house. There, he lived wildly and loved to hide in holes, in dress rooms, behind trees and places where nobody could find him, to be alone and have his visions in his mind. He had many visions of his future life and music melodies.

He would dream often about a so beautiful blue eyes golden hair fairy princess and had many visions about her...He loved to touch the hedgehogs around the house and look at the ant's kingdom and also watch all sort of yellow bees. He would often stare at the fields full of red poppies, watching the butter flies around him, lady bugs always came to him, and always made wishes when they would fly away from his hands, and when they would be sinking in the pools, he would save them and help them fly again.

Down, not so far from the house, a source of water was flowing, where nearby was a water pool with frogs and their baby doyers, that was the way the baby frogs were called. Two hundred walks far, a smaller water pool with besides a pomegranate tree who would give his fruits in summer. Close to there were mandarin trees and the biggest orange tree of the island. Farther down, he would go alone visit the bats hiding in the unreachable caves and stayed long time in that mysterious place having visions of his future.

There somewhere around the house, a little cave hidden by a shrub would fascinate him. He always imagined there lived a strange creature of one of his elf drawing books.

In the surroundings of the double house, he loved to look at a plant where the delightful vision coming from nowhere looking like a light fairy princess with blue eyes, remained in his mind. She would appear and would stay hours present in his day time visions.

One day he was playing with his first wheel tool and his older brother pushed him in to the roses. He had all his face scratched and on his throat a few spines. His mother brought him to the big room where he was born, it was the old kitchen where used to be made the bread, where she took away the spines from his throat, telling him "When you were born it was as easy as breaking an egg..."

Once they were living in the mountains and with his older brother they were on a stiff field with a girl of their class and one small dog came to barb at him when he was sitting on the grass and for a long time his brother was laughing at him while the dog was attacking him. He did not have good connection with most of dogs. He was very reserved and would not communicate much with other kids, and spent his time alone living in his melodies dream.

He learnt first to play the harmonica with no body teaching him and he made a drum with an orange garbage bin, he would put it upside down to hit on the bottom which was then the top once on his legs becoming his first rhythm drum. With his own hands, he built himself a wooden string tool without strings, with which he was sometimes going to the nearby around trees imagining himself playing it in front of crowds...

Then later he had a real one with plastic strings that was his brother's at first and became his then. His father after bought him a red tronic metal string tool, with which he would spend all his time making the steel strings sound.

One day with his wheel tool he was around his mother and his brother. In the path to go down to the village there was an enormous stiff hill and suddenly when he was going down that stiff path the brakes were not responding and the wheel tool was taking speed. He did not react, and found himself with so much speed that he couldn't stop when at the swerve his wheel tool with him on it jumped a few walks away and found himself knocking his head and back on the ground. When he opened the eyes after time unconscious, his mother and his brother were laughing while his back was in a pain, they did not seem to care for his fall. Many years after, he thought about it again and he realized his brother may have sabotaged his brakes before he took the hill because he knew he was jalousie of him.

In those times of history everyone watched a plastic box with people inside talking or moving. His mother allowed them to watch that plastic box only once a week and she called that box #the stupid box# probably because the people inside did not know you, and you could not speak with them but only listen to them and they did not care if you like them or not...

Soon they moved to another kingdom to live, where he had to learn a new language and at school, he had to also learn to make sound the flute. He was strange for others because he kept his hair long, so he was often rejected, and violently attacked by other teenage who could not understand him. But in music class, when he would start bowing sounds with his flute for exams, all the kids of his class would remain silent, with admiration because his sounds were so inspiring. As he was a very shy boy and refused to kiss girls because he knew they were not The fairy princess of his dreams, other kids would say he was not a true boy but a girlyboy.

In the new house where they were living there were many crickets in summer time coming from the field in front. One day he found hundreds of them in the hall of his room and he was afraid of them so he scratched all the crickets with heavy books. He felt fear and did not understand the crickets wanted to be his friends...

CHAPTER 2
HE GETS HURT BY A WOMAN

He also was the best of his class in the most famous language at that time, so his father sent him to one kingdom where they spoke that language and there in the family where he stayed, the mother forced him to do things he did not want to do, but they created music together. He was so much practicing every day his plastic string wooden music tool that he was damaging his right arm, having already back problems at a so young age. He loved on daughter of the family for who he wrote a song called Thought of Spring which was her nick name. She was not the fairy princess of his visions, but they shared love for the time he stayed there until her mother and her father forbade her to see him. There he bought a wooden flute made from that land, and loved to blow on it, and blew melodies to Spring.

When he came back his father, he stopped going to school and stayed in his room instead practicing his singing. He was transforming himself opening his throat, until one morning some phenomenon happened inside of him. He felt transformed and his throat was making more powerful sounds. He was then going to the big village walking everywhere chanting ancient singing while hitting in rhythm his right hand on his chest. People would not understand his new behavior. He was feeling powerful forces from somewhere else and felt like being in other power forces in the earth but his brothers were suffering from the shame of his behavior. So his father told him to go more to the nature alone, so he picked that wooden flute he brought from that faraway land and was blowing peace sounds from it to everyone he would cross and to the nature and the birds.

His father then brought him to see his best friend who knew the position of the lotus and he was taught that position and was told to make that position as much as he wanted. So he was going to the nature with his wooden flute siting on the nature land listening to the peace of the birds and making the sounds of his wooden flute for them. He sometimes took frogs with his hands and snails he found in the nature and showed to kids around the village all the different types of animals he would find.

He was a music dreamer...and loved the most to put snails on his arms and show it to others.

One day he found a little bird with a damaged wing and took care of him but his father was telling him he was a ridiculous idiot to take care of a little damaged bird so he decided to send him back to that women whom he did not love or like so he would make again music with her. He had found who he was inside of himself, so he wouldn't let that woman force him to make what he didn't want to, so she sent him back to his father because he would not do anymore what she would tell him to.

CHAPTER 3
THE ENCHANTER FINDS THE
DIMENTION OF THE ANGELS

He came back in a strange state of mind and his father bought him a big heavy stick eucalyptus with which he learned to make sounds with continuous breathing. He would blow on that stick for hours in summer time. That is how he became good friends with the crickets he had smashed when he was young. They were making the rhythms for his big stick sounds. He realized that the crickets were good musician drummers. They were every afternoon making music together and he found peace inside going every day to the nature alone singing sacred chantings, but unlucky the girlfriend of one of his brothers was repeating to him "You will be a tramp, if you don't work you will be a tramp" all the time "You will see people will tell you, you are a tramp, and they will talk about you just like a tramp" She annoyed him until his harmony misbalanced and got broken. Lost in his mind he had no strength to live in harmony on the nature anymore and took again the path of stress going back to school and worrying for the future life. He was working hard in a restaurant cleaning the table cutlery, the large casseroles and the floors to earn coins. He would fall down and hurt his ankle, understanding unconsciously that he was not in his path life.

He also worked in gardens and many little jobs living lot of stress. He tried to work hard for the exams but he knew unconsciously, that all what he was studding was in vain so he started to sit on the lotus position again on his bed for more than five hours every night. One night he rose with his unphysical body to a dimension where he saw his seven spirits when another power came in to him and his being was tele transported to a higher dimension where all was light. A pure being dressed in pure white like the sun or like the moon, appeared in front of him and he was scared. It was the most shocking experience he had ever had. After his nonphysical body coming back down to the earth, he was sure and had understood he had seen the heavens and knew the meaning of life and what was after life. He knew for sure there was a heavens waiting for the virtuous beings. He kept going to school but he was not anymore the same and was having visions of his future life traveling in the streets.

At the end of the school year, he failed his exams as he knew would happen but he had seen the dimension of the heavens, the higher power of the light, and knew pertinently what was the real truth of all religions. He had hurt more his arm by writing the lessons for philosophy classes and by practicing his string music tools so much, but that was the hard path he had, to arrive to his knowledge then.

CHAPTER 4
HE LEAVES HIS FATHER'S HOME

He felt detachment from everything and also from his family whom was harassing him because he had failed and wouldn't do anything but walk on the mountains alone and see other power forces.

He decided he had to leave his family and went away with a bag and walked and walked until arriving to a kingdom where he started to live in a cave. He also often slept besides a small pool on a short size wall and to his mind came many dreams of making his music for all the people there. But soon he realized he was not living his deepest dream and got revolted inside and angry at every one there and left that place to look for his deep dream.

He then lived traveling on the streets, working sometimes in the fields picking oranges, pumpkins, grapes and melons to earn some coins to be able to buy what he needed for his survival life. He would often eat apples from the wild trees and berries and cherries when the generous trees were in his way. Once he was picking the olives to earn some coins and during the night he was sleeping inside the little room where were the pipes to water the trees, it was smelling like strong minerals, he felt a presence from the wall and there suddenly was a big grey lizard. Strangely he was not falling gripping the grey wall and he was amazed. In his youth he had only seen very small lizards and that big one fulfilled him with happiness and peace.

His meetings with wild animals were his biggest peace and his favorite ceremony of life but he couldn't play anymore his string music tool, his shoulder and his entire arm had been too damaged because of so much practicing, so his music passion was trapped in his handicapped arm. He kept his dream in one corner of his mind though thinking one day he will find what he came to search for in this earth.

He was realizing he never took the time to love himself when he was growing and the attitude to himself was wrong hurting himself letting the aggressive outside world damage his own heart and his mind. He consciously understood his excessive string tool practicing was his big shyness towards princesses, so he was learning to approach them on the streets where ever he went and also to treat with them. He never had had a girlfriend princess, he was still too shy, but he spoke with more princesses than anybody in the earth. He was learning to be always alone discovering his heart and the trust in the higher power, trusting on the day after day because he had no work and no stable living place and no stable life. But he was living in a perfect relationship with himself.

CHAPTER 5
FIRST TIME HE EXPERIENCES THE HURT IN LOVE
THE ENCHANTER OF THE FLUTE SHARES HIS ROOM WITH MICES

He met one day a princess called Marion who he loved but they hurt each other's hearts very strongly. For five years he could not love other princesses, his heart was too damaged. He looked to work as a steel builder because he loved the burning steel smell and also steel rust taste but they did not allow him to learn steel worker, so he had to keep looking for other works. He was living in a very big town in a little room which was the house of the duke of that area hundreds years ago. He could afford that room because the kingdom administration would provide five hundred and two hundred thirty coins monthly to anyone who did not have an actual work.

There, he was meeting many princesses but none of them were The fairy princess of his dreams. Sometimes, when he was with some of them, some mice would appear besides the river and also on the grass in the parks and the princesses would totally freak out, it was the sign for him that they were not the one for his heart because he loved the little mice so much. He enjoyed the dark nights and loved the autumn seasons and was most of the time alone because he was totally allergic to perfume and also paper smoke, and would not stand artificial light from people's living place while most of the people were either wearing perfume either smoking paper sticks, either submitting them self's to arterial light in their living place.

One day he bought a western steel string tool and went to look for the princess Marion crossing half of the continent, where he found a ferret and was going to show him to the princess Marion because she loved ferrets as he did but, when he arrived to that town Marion refused to see him. So he was playing his western steel music tool and that ferret was all the time biting his hands. As she did not want to see him and the ferret, he was leaving. When he was packing his belongings strangely that ferret opened the cage's door and went back to the nature. When he went to pick the cage he saw the cage empty.

When he arrived back the town he was living, his room was taken by someone else, so he was transferred to another smaller room where he met little mice living in the holes of the walls. And he remembered his psychic friend's companion taught him how to make real bread and he learnt in his little living place alone kneading the dough experiencing many ways until he understood how the bread dough worked. He also found the passion of juggling with two full bottles of wine with which he was training besides the river every afternoon.

He sometimes was buying music tools but would give them away to strangers for free because his shoulder and arm would hurt too much when trying to play for a long time. He was unhappy there, he felt he was getting old and in his life his dream was never was arriving. He felt he could never have the courage to go travel on the streets again and he would finish his life with a routine like everyone in the earth. The only satisfaction he had was his little mice coming to visit him at night when him sleeping on his bed. He would listen to them eat his plastic bags at night making soft sounds. They were eating also his wheat for his bread but strangely the mice never touched the cheese that he left for them. Sometimes the little mice would come sing softy in very high melodies behind his pillow enchanting his mind. He was living simply with no work, no princess, making his bread and feeding himself with home-made bread, sault and butter or sault and oil. Unhappy he learnt to live very humble life, singing his melodies to himself with a soft voice walking everywhere in that big town with nostalgic feelings. Years were passing by and he didn't know how to change his life. . .

CHAPTER 6
THE ENCHANTER OF THE FLUTE DISCOVERS THE GIFT OF SPEAKING WITH KIDS ON THE STREETS AND HE LIVES WITH MICES

Step after step he was discovering a gift, while walking around the town, when he saw kids crying, he would talk to them with a soft child voice and the kids would become calm and quiet, and would look at him with admiration... Their parents were not able to treat them with kindness, they thought they had to be strict with them. Some parents would be afraid of a stranger talking to their kids but most of them would thank him for calming down their kids crying... So he chose to never go losing his peace with princess who would smoke paper sticks or drink, in order to stay in harmony and console the kids on the streets. The princess who liked to drink of smoke and play seduction games making their choice but the kids were too fragile and too little to be able to choose for them self's.

One day in the middle of the winter he heard from his neighbor that everyone living in that old little building were complaining because of the mice entering in their rooms and the owner came to warn that they were going to put poison in the holes of the walls to kill the mice, so he got even more unhappy, where nobody would really understand what he loved and enjoyed. They didn't know that the mice were good singers, they were too busy talking to their plastic boxes to notice that, and too busy smoking a paper stick in their mouth to understand the life of the little mice, but he knew it was useless to explain them, most of the people at that time thought mice were dirty and full of illnesses, they didn't know the illness came from their own mind and then their mind would create illness in their body and life.

His neighbor was an old mean man and smoked cigars. From the corridor the smoke could enter in his room from the spaces of the doors. So he was sleeping in winter all night long with the opened window in order to breathe fresh air, but his blanket was not warm enough. After the mean neighbor was opening the window too, so the smoke of his neighbor's cigar was entering from the open space around the not secure door and also from the window, so fresh air was no longer coming from outside. He was trapped, he could not have heat or fresh air to breath fluently. So he bought an elegant wind gold music tool and travelled far away in the neighbor kingdom and left that living place.

Then he thought he should have taken the mice with him to save them from this fearful neighbors who didn't recognize their singing talent. He felt like he abandoned his friends and always regretted to not have taken them with him.

CHAPTER 7
HE LEAVES TRAVELING AGAIN
SEARCHING FOR HIS DEEP DREAM

He was in that enormous town blowing his golden music tool and getting coins to pay his room in hotels and there he met Irene a princess he loved but when she went to visit her sister faraway, he was waiting for her and another princess wanted to kiss him, he stayed loyal. When his princess Irene came back, she announced him she was in love with the princess girl living in her sister's living place. His shoulder then started to hurt again because of playing every day his golden music tool so he went back to sleep on the streets, but found a black bird flute and was sending his melodies to the huge big long garden of that enormous town crossing the enormous vast park of thousands of walks long every day. He was the flute nomad of that nature part of the town but his left palm thumb had gotten infected by the tension of playing his bird flute because of his old electrical damage coming back which was creating tension in his left palm thumb while playing his golden elegant music tool. He was trying to calm down the thumb pain in the water storage of the cemetery where he was sleeping, but the winter was over and the spring had warmed up the water storage not being cold enough to release the pain of his hand. He abandoned his bird flute and the big town he loved and kept traveling feeling the pain feeling like a needle planted in his palm thumb.

When he arrived back where he was living in the small room with the mice, he was given by the princess Kora Sen, a little ferret, very nice, called Amazon. Amazon never bit anybody. He was leaving him on the streets and watching him from twenty walks. All the kids would go pick Amazon in their arms, and Amazon would go around their body. And when princesses would pick him up, he would enter inside the dresses of all the princesses taking him with their arms. Everyone loved Amazon.

One day they went together with Amazon for an adventure in the mountains, camping beside a lake. Amazon slashed in one of the two sleeping bags, so he had to clean it in the lake and put it to dry on a tree. The same day when they were coming from the store eating from a glass jar, the very cold wind arrived suddenly from the north of the earth. His fingers got so cold that he had to throw fast to the floor the glass jar to not let his fingers freeze. He ran to his camp to be protected from the cold wind, but they had only one dry sleeping bag. That night he was almost freezing while Amazon was not aware of the danger, but they survived.

A few days after, he left Amazon under a worm wool cover he found in an abandoned house where they slept. In the morning the tramp went to take him, Amazon was totally trembling. He felt so guilty realizing he let Amazon sleep alone in the cold. And some strange people opened the door and warned him of the unappropriated manners for them to sleep there because the property belonged to a religious group.

Amazon was then very week and wouldn't move so much but the tramp managed to take a double room living place to stay in wormer with Amazon. He bought another steel string tool and he was playing so much that his left arm got hurting again but there they had the cold lake so he went to the lake to put his arm in the cold water for around one hour. It was middle of winter and the lake was more than cold enough. While his hand was on the cold water, he was feeling like a strong electrical needle on the thumb palm until the needle disappeared and felt released. He realized then that the lake had healed his arm and absorbed the needle of electricity hurting his left arm. They only stayed two weeks in that room cause Amazon and the tramp were both true adventurers .They got driven again back to the big town and met a handicapped prince always sitting on a wheel chair who owned a little ferret princess who needed love from Amazon. So he left Amazon with her make his life. He loved his ferret but they were not really compatible and he was happy that Amazon finally found the big love. Amazon and the princess ferret were all day sleeping making an eight making a ying and yang one over each other as a united love.

He kept traveling alone and sometime later he bought a steel string tool and was going around all the towns making melodies sounds sliding water glasses or bottles on the music tool's steel strings singing for the people who he would meet. He was traveling in towns sleeping close to castles and in many different places and meeting many nice princesses. He would sometimes try to save the snails from been crashed by wheel machines but they were so many of them that he could end up getting crashed. He found himself arrived in one very nice town and the first night he saw a wild weasel close to the little river in the old part of the town and became happy and satisfied. The tramp also really loved the wild weasels even if he could not approach them.

CHAPTER 8
HE FINDS HIS MAGICAL DRUM

Sometime after, he bought a wheel machine and arrived to a big town where many people would make fire art. There he found in a store a big heavy magical drum and loved it, so he bought it with some coins he had been given by his family. He was then traveling with the magical drum driving his wheel machine but he wasn't receiving many coins when hitting his magical drum on the streets. Then he decided to buy a caring wheel tool to carry his magical drum because he got tired of being carried with his magical drum by his wheel machine. He was riding his wheel tool with brakes not correctly adjusted, he fell and broke his left arm, so he could not leave with the wheel tool broken in two pieces. So he left the magical drum in his brother's house, and left with his broken arm until arrived to the capital of a kingdom. He saw there besides a bin, a mouse totally still and got worried for her and remembered he abandoned his singer mice friends in his little room years ago. He took the little mouse in his hands, he made a box for her and brought her with him. The little mouse couldn't move, she had been shocked by the sounds of loud wheel machines. He was taking care of her traveling with her until she was moving all over because she was healed and jumped from his hands moving her legs fast running back to the nature forest. Pride was inside of his heart when showing the little mouse to kids, but she went her wild life so he continued traveling alone with his broken arm.

In the town after, the first evening when he arrived, he saw a fox and followed the fox, but the fox was too fast so he couldn't become his friend.

He followed his path, crossed the sea with a boat and arrived to a kingdom where people were strange and not very friendly but he met a woman who told him that he could have her little house or even burn it if he decided to, or do whatever he wanted with it because she didn't care at all anymore. That little house had one room where was a small wooden stove,, one kitchen where was a very old wood oven being used to cook one century earlier, one little place way smaller than a room where he could work making handmade shoes and a place in the entrance where he could build a shower and also on the roof was a space with a bed but there were living bees and he got bitten, but he liked to feel the bees poison on his muscles. Ten walks from the little house you could find a source of water. Apparently there was a lynx as he was told by that woman, but the lynx never showed up. He was happy feeling lost in the world with a broken arm alone in peace in his little house around the nature and the trees, but he was sleeping all the time and his left shoulder was hurting, hurting because he wouldn't move. So he left that place he had been given so he would be in movement and then his arm would heal.

In the capital of that kingdom, he finally met some nice people who introduced to him the doctor Stephan who injected right away in his shoulder a liquid to heal faster his arm without asking him anything in exchange. In two minutes his arm was almost recovered and he could continue exploring the many places he hadn't been.

He crossed again the darkest sea he ever had seen with a boat and arrived to a small kingdom where all the princesses were very nice. He liked that place, and many of his favorite birds were there around the long gardens, the black crows. The pigeons were absent, the kind of birds making annoying smell where ever he slept. There he started to learn one of the main languages spoken in that kingdom and when he knew the first language, he started learning the second one.

He had learnt the basic of two new languages. He was happy there, and bought many music tools with the coins his father left his brother for him before dying. It was a plastic strings tool, a golden trumpet, another silver elegant tool and another tronic steel string tool, and also a harmonica. He was living in a boat a friend had found for him and he had a nice princess Agathe who he loved but he knew deep inside she was not The fairy princess of his dreams, and felt he needed to go get his magical drum to his brother.

CHAPTER 9
HE FINDS A WHEEL TOOL AND STARTS TRAVELING WITH IT

So he left the boat, as his intuition was telling him and crossed the continent to go back to the kingdom of his brother, where in the middle of the continent he stopped in the capital of a kingdom and started to learn also that kingdom's language, when he spoke to a princess hairdresser who showed him where was an abandoned wheel tool and told him he could have it and so crossed the other half of the continent with that wheel tool.

When he arrived to the kingdom where lived his brother, one friend helped him buy a carrier wheel tool to carry his big magical drum and arrived to his brother's living place with it. He put the big magical drum in his wheel tool carrier, worked in his good friend's house building and gardening for some days and started his big trip. He crossed many castles and many rivers and met a steel worker who built stronger his magical drum carrier wheel tool with his steel abilities and gave him another wheel tool but the brakes of that wheel tool broke in half way. He was then riding without brakes but the land he was crossing was flat. He did some more thousands of thousands walks until he arrived to a town called Kaunas and he heard in his mind —I'll be back here'- He followed his goal and arrived back to the kingdom where he had left all his music tools.

There he started making handmade shoes again but blowing in the cold winter his silver elegant music tool in an under road but he was not very successful and didn't receive much coins and he was not much happy in that kingdom anymore, like he was at the beginning.

But one afternoon he met a pretty princess called Dasha and they agreed that he would go visit her in Kaunas. So he organized his departure and hid his music tools in a friend princess's cave in Doma, it was a place where people could go and sleep for twelve coins or more. He made nice handmade sandals for her on her birthday and she gave him a wooden heart with the colors of the neighbor kingdom and then left to that kingdom for the town Kaunas.

CHAPTER 10
HE ARRIVES TO THE KINGDOM OF THE FAIRY PRINCESS

With his wheel carrier, he only carried to Kaunas his little moon drum, his trumpet and his harmonica in order to have a lighter carrier. In the first day he arrived that town, lot of people were selling handmade tools in the main street, all sort of tools and clothes, some body was selling moon drums...

The first princess he met, explained him where he could find Dasha's school so he went there to check if he would meet her, and he saw her the Monday at one in the afternoon. Dasha told him that they will meet but with no other details but she seemed more scared than anything.

He was sleeping in the big natural park called Angelinas which was on a hill. For a few days, he was trying to make sound his trumpet and sleeping in that park but only struggling sounds were coming out.

The first night there he met an old man with a hat on his head and a steel string tool on his shoulder, he was under the wheel machine path. That place had been scripted the name of Transition. The third day, he met a painter who also blew on his elegant silver music tool with who he played jamming sounds with his little moon drum. And the painter invited him to clean his clothes and rest in his house.

The first evening he went to blow on his trumpet under the wheel machines path in the Transition. He managed to make sounds but only a few nice sounds which was enough to make him happy. He only received on his gloves laying on the floor four coins, it was not much, but it made him feel satisfied. He started to go every evening under the road transition to blow his trumpet and receive a few coins on his gloves.

He decided then to make again handmade shoes because the painter had many leather pieces which his father who was a tailor had left him before passing away, and he started making handmade pink boots for the painter and brown shoes for himself.

The painter told him he had the dream of making nicer his house building a painting room on the yard land besides the house. As the music tramp was a hard worker, he went to buy a shovel and was moving the yard soil with the shovel with intense effort creating a very nice yard for the painter to welcome people who could come see his paintings.

In the afternoon he would work hard in the yard and in the evening he would go blow his trumpet under the road Transition.

He became a music beggar, blowing sounds and melodies waiting people would drop coins at his glove laying on the floor...

The first week in that town, the music beggar was blowing his trumpet, and he saw passing by a prince and said to him. "Hello I see a steel string tool in your life" He had the gift to see things without seeing with the eyes...and the prince answered "I don't have a steel string tool, no" But the music beggar insisted "Well I see a string tool in your life" He managed to see the blue steel string tool of his princess...After the prince said "Well my princess has one but it is not me" and went closer to the music beggar and told him "Actually my princess wants to learn to play better her steel string music tool and I want to pay some body to teach her..." As the music beggar was able to play the string tools very well, he told the prince "Oh I play very well string tool instruments" So the prince offered him to teach to his princess because he wanted to offer her string tool lessons for her birthday. The prince brought the music beggar to his living place and spoke about the meaning of life...While going up the stairs to his living place, the prince told the music beggar "My princess is a doctor" They had after a conversation about princesses because the music beggar told the prince he came to this kingdom meet a princess called Dasha and as his home was the streets. The prince wanted to inform him how to get princesses "You know you have to show to the princesses that they will have the comfort want and the security if they come with you" The music beggar was a passionate person so he thought a princess should go with a prince because she really loved the inside heart and mind of a prince and not for what he owned or the comfort he would provide to the princess. He didn't get enchanted by the prince's thoughts but he did not comment anything because he noticed that the prince was limited minded.

The music beggar accidently talked about Jesus Christ the one king who came once in the earth, and the prince did not accept that Jesus was the king and got offended asking "And just Jesus and why not others?" The music beggar tried to explain him that not everyone had the same courage and every being had different glory and that we won our dignity by our courage...

He could not speak freely as the prince felt attacked loosing peace because of his trust on the king Jesus words. They were eating when he explained to the prince that himself had seen to the highest of the light world and the prince told him "Hum you are a good person" but the music beggar had a blurry vision that he would fall in love with his princess and he said "Well good person, what if I fall in love with your princess?"

And the prince said "We will see what will happen" Not much time passed that suddenly somebody opened the door, and it was her his fairy princess, she went right away to the bathroom. When she was back, and went to sit be sides Her prince and then they talked. The music beggar told them again that he met a very nice princess who lived in their kingdom who he came to meet. The princess told him that she played the flute, but the music beggar did not really understand well what she meant because Her prince had told him that she was a doctor. As The princess and Her prince danced often together, they told the music beggar that they liked to move dancing. The music beggar was embarrassed because he found The princess was the most beautiful princess he ever met, and was hard for him to not look at her...He then asked to play her blue steel string tool. She accepted to let him try it, so he grabbed his drinking glass with water from the table and sang some words for her making sound her steel strings sliding sounds with the water glass, but she didn't know those words were for her. When he had finished playing her string music tool, he couldn't look at her because Her prince was asking him questions. Going to the restroom he escaped the situation because he could not affirm himself in front of her...

When he came back The princess was on her knees kissing Her prince...The music beggar felt so hurt like if a spear penetrated his heart and tears were in his eyes like if his predestined princess had left him for another prince. So he said with a sad heart "I have to go" and they stopped kissing and joined him to the door where the music beggar avoiding his pain said "Thanks for listening to my water glass sounds and steel strings" Her prince made loop the princess holding her hand like dancing her body and said "We also create sounds with our dance" The music beggar felt another spear in his heart when seeing the prince touch her hands making her body loop but he just said "I am going now" And Her prince told him "You come again soon eat with us..." holding The princess with his arms...The music beggar woke out and the prince closed the door.

Soon looking in the painter's music tool room, he found a plastic flute and asked to borough it, and the painter accepted, so he started to blow that flute in evenings...

One day during the same week while the music beggar was speaking with someone in the Transition, The princess and Her prince appeared from the right, they were coming from their dance. The music beggar was so impressed by her because she was so beautiful for his mind but, he couldn't look at her and Her prince said "We come from dancing" The beggar of music did not know what to say so he just said "Waw...you are tall princess" And Her prince added "Yes she is a tall princess" The music beggar felt some love for her but didn't know what to say so he just said "I don't like dancing" Surprised they retorted "Oh you don't like dancing?" And Her prince added "Ah, I see you are a lazy person" So he answered "Well not really, I just don't like moving my legs, or maybe just for tango romantic dance in last option" When he said those words he imagined himself dancing with her a romantic tango dance... As they were tired from their dance training they did not stay longer and went home.

An evening the music beggar was speaking with the first princess he spoke in Kaunas, when The princess and Her prince appeared, and he was cold with them. He didn't know how to act in front of her and was angry because he wished to have an as beautiful princess as her but he did not...

The music beggar was blowing his trumpet every evenings feeling the joy of life and in the main street of the town he met a princess and tried to be her prince kissing her because The princess had already Her prince but he became unhappy because he didn't take the time to think that he loved The princess.

CHAPTER 11
THE ENCHANTER SPEAKS ALONE
WITH HIS FAIRY PRINCESS

One afternoon he fell in the stares of the painter's house and twisted his ankle and then realized that he was in love with The princess...

In the evening with the twisted ankle, he was very late out blowing his trumpet and suddenly he felt a soft feeling coming from his right side and lost control of his melodies, stopped blowing his trumpet and turned his head to the right...There was The princess alone approaching towards him and stopped in front of him.

She first said "I was thinking about you..." And he asked "You were thinking about me?" She answered with peace "Yes, when I heard your trumpet sound and I knew it was you" And he replied "Ah..." He didn't know what to say...He was surprised and embarrassed, and she asked "How is it going with the princess you came here to meet?" And he answered "Tomorrow I will go in front of her school hitting on my little moon drum and I may see her" He was feeling shy so he started to talk about his trumpet hiding his thoughts. She left saying "I am tired now, I want to go" He felt boring to her, and unsatisfaction fulfilled him.

The day after in the morning he went to hit his little mon drum in front of the school to see the princess Dasha who he came to visit, to check if he would meet her but she did not appear. That was not the real problem, the problem was that all day long hitting his little moon drum, he only could think about The princess...

The same day before the sun sat, Her prince appeared and insisting making him come to his living place to eat, where they spoke about The princess...The music beggar asked him "So you said your princess is a doctor and you an architect?" And he replied "I am an architect, and she wants to be a kid's teacher" The music beggar understood then why she had told him she played the flute...to enchant the kids...

In the evening in the Transition he was but this time blowing the harmonica instead of the trumpet, when suddenly he felt soft strange feelings coming from the right side and was out of control of his melodies. He stopped blowing his harmonica and turned his head to the right and The princess was there approaching to him and stopped in front of him and he was fulfilled by her peace... The princess spoke first "I was thinking about you" And the music beggar said "I was thinking about Dasha and also about you because I felt you coming" He was wondering why he should look for the princess Dasha if he was in love with her and he asked her "Yesterday you told me you were thinking about me before you heard my trumpet or when you heard my trumpet?" She answered "Well when I heard your trumpet, I knew it was you" So he was even more confused and it remained not clear in his mind but he did not ask any more about it. And so they spoke more... She asked him "So how was your meeting with your princess?" He explained her "I didn't cross her" And he added "I have a problem, I always rethink and keep in mind for a few days the bad experiences..." Hearing his thought, she looked worried and asked him "So it was for you a bad experience to speak with me?" And he answered "No, not at all, but I was thinking about you all day long and that is a problem" And he was so gently tendered by her that he could not help and more words melted from his mind "And you are so pretty..." while he was looking at her pretty face. She then told him "What you are saying makes me feel very good, I have many complexes about myself" and she asked him again "What are you going to do with your princess?" He was trapped because he did not care about the other princess anymore, he was in love with her but how to announce that, he could not tell her right away, and he answered "I am going to write her a letter and go to her school again on Monday at one, I know she finishes at one o'clock" And almost interrupting him she said "Oh...I would love somebody writes me letters but nobody does..." So the music beggar said "I could write you letters in the language of my kingdom but you would not understand..." So she said like charmed "I could translate them..."

She then expressed how she was "I am an old fashion princess, my prince likes new things but I don't like it so much..." The music beggar also liked old things so he said

"I also like old things, old houses, old wheel tools, old wheel machines, where I was living for one year before coming here, there are nice places in the capital where to ride calmly old wheel tools" He had at that exact moment the dream to ride with her in the capital he lived before arriving to her kingdom. He asked her "So you are studying to be a doctor?" And she answered "No I am studding to be a child teacher" He was trying to understand "Your prince told me his girlfriend was a doctor" So she informed him "The previous princess he had was a doctor that is why" It was confusing for him but he started to talk about music to her, expressing to her "I see you with a travers flute" She said "I would like to try" So he asked her "Would you like to have one?" She answered "Yes I would like to and I would also like to have a wooden flute…" She didn't like the plastic flute she was forced to use during her teaching lessons, because The princess loved wood and dislike plastic. In his mind it was clear he was going to buy her a traverse flute and a wooden flute as she wished, but he did not tell her of course. It was going to be her birthday gift. He then changed the conversation trying to hide it so it could be a surprise "I am going to buy a mute part for my trumpet to make more romantic sounds" And without interest she told him "I have to go, I want to go home, we will meet this next days later after my duty work if you are here, and after the end of this week I stop working, I don't like the duties I am doing" And while she was leaving, she was turning her head towards him, as if she liked him.

Now he knew she wanted to have a wooden flute because she wanted to be a kid teacher and she needed a real wooden flue to make sleep the kids. He went back to the painter's living place, laid on the bed and his heart started beating very strong. He stood up and went to take a pencil and a white paper and wrote to her the first letter in his kingdom language expressing how strong he felt for her and fell sleep on the couch. In the middle of night, the painter arrived, entered in the room where he was and started screaming "I give you three days to pack all your tools and go away from my house! I am tired of you!

I am tired of life! I don't want to hurt you but I want you to go away from my house!" The music beggar was very fast, it took him not three days but a three minutes to gather all his music tools and prepare his wheel tool carrier. Before leaving he put back the flute he borrowed where he found it and went to camp the rest of hours left before the sun rose in the morning.

In the evening, he was waiting outside the Transition for The princess with the letter in his hands. He waited until very late after midnight but she did not pass by. He didn't understand why she did not come by as she told him she would after her duty work. He rode his wheel tool crossing on bridge arriving in to the island in-between two flows of rivers and slept under two crying trees...

The day after, he was again after midnight waiting until very late in the underground transition to see if The princess would pass by there, but she did not. He went to old town with his wheel tool look for her but he did not find her, so he thought she would already be home, he joined the crying tree and slept again there.

The day after he crossed Her prince who told him "The princess and I are going to another kingdom to buy stones for my glory kingdom, and we will be away for one week"

That day the music beggar went alone to buy in a music tool store one plastic flute for him and went back to the neighbor kingdom where he was living before to bring his big magical space drum and his other music tools to the kingdom of The princess.

When he was back, one evening he was with another friend, when The princess and Her prince passed by...Then he managed to ask her "Why I did not see you after your duties the last two days of your work?" And she replied "I went back home another way" He was very disappointed but didn't show his feelings and tried to pretend it did not affect him. Then Her prince told him "My princess is going to dance with a short dress to show her moves to make enjoyment, other princes" The music beggar got worried and his mind was hurt so The princess said "He is joking" They spoke some more when a tall prince approached wanting to shake his hand and the prince's hand but also took the hand of The princess and kissed her hand. Her prince did not care about His princess's hand being kissed by somebody else but the music beggar was mad crazy out of mind and out of control and said with worried emotions "That's not something he is supposed to do kissing the hand of a princess that he doesn't even know!" After this event they spoke some more about nothing much important...The music beggar was so nervous that he was talking about things without meaning or without sense and hey got bored so they left.

The next day the music beggar was hitting his magical drum...and he felt a strange soft feeling coming from his right side and turned his head to the right, The princess and Her prince were walking to his way...When he saw The princess, his heart started beating strongly, inspired he kept hitting his magical drum and closed his eyes. When The princess and Her prince arrived in front of him, the music beggar felt magi inside hitting his magical drum, The princess was in front of him feeling his magical melodies. She closed her eyes, with the music beggar, they were together in another dimension time both alone feeling in their peace kingdom power... The music beggar opened and closed the eyes and noticed Her prince was not with them he was just looking around his wheel tool and his streets tools. He saw The princess remained closed eyes staying in his garden melodies, like if everything around had disappeared and him and her only then existed.

When he stopped hitting his magical drum he asked them "How would you dance on my power sounds" And Her prince made her loop dancing three moves but the music beggar did not feel good seeing that so he couldn't hit his magical drum anymore. As they were just passing by to go buy some fruits for their home, they entered in the fruit store. When they had finished getting what they needed, they passed by him again without stopping or saying anything to him. . .

The day after in the morning surrounded by countless soft fluffy dandelions, the beggar wrote with tears in his heart the first long poem for The princess.

In the late afternoon when he was sitting with another princess he knew called Ugne, The princess and Her prince passed by with the bag of fruits they were carrying from the store to their living place. This time was the first time they didn't stop by him and it was the first time also that the music beggar saw The princess in short dress. He got angry because of her dressing that way. He disliked to see her dressed that way following Her prince.

CHAPTER 12
HE FINDS OUT WHO IS THE FAIRY PRINCESS

In the morning after, on the grass under his crying trees around the fluffy dandelions, he wrote with his heart crying another very long poem for The princess in his kingdom language...

In the same day during the afternoon, the sun was very present and powerful, he was in his knees in the presence of the higher forces in a prayer building and asked to the King Jesus to speak to The princess.

And when the music beggar was blowing his flute just in front of where The princess lived which was where he made up melodies every day. He felt a strange feeling coming from his back and couldn't control anymore his melodies, stopped blowing his flute and turned his head to the left, The princess was walking to him, when she was right in front of him she told him "Wait, I come in a few minutes"

The music beggar's heart was beating so strongly and he was feeling a way that he never felt before. Some short time after The princess appeared with two lemons on her hands, she offered one to him and kept one for her...The music beggar then asked her "So you said you would like somebody would write you letters?" And she answered "Yes I did say so" So he asked her "I wrote two poems for you, do you want them?" And she answered "Yes I want them" So he handed to her the poems and she took them with her small hand...The poems were in his kingdom language, they were two very long poems, long like three pages full of words both sides.

The music beggar had already ordered from his kingdom the magical wooden flute for her, so he spoke about her flute, and he noticed she had three dots under one eye of the color light blue and asked her "You painted three blue dots under your eye?" And she answered "Yes, do you know what it means?" He didn't know, so he answered "No, I don't." And she then told him "It's a fairy mark..." And he enjoyed her childish style so he said "I love it..." She was so pleased and he fell totally enchanted and thought she was a fairy and started to feel she was The fairy princess of his life...

She also told him that she worked hard and she did not get paid for seven hundred coins worth duties, and that she wanted to go to the mountains but she could not because she had not enough coins to go. The beggar didn't comment about it because he thought they were going to go together to the mountains very soon, now that he knew she was The fairy princess of his dreams. And he told her "I don't like princesses wearing short dresses" And The fairy princess said "I also don't but I am learning to be a woman and let the man pay for me"

She also said that she would like to learn three more languages which were spoken in the south of their continent and as the music beggar knew two of them he told her "It is with me that you are going to learn them, I will teach them to you, you will see" But as Her prince had promised her they will learn together those languages, she thought she will learn them with Her prince. She couldn't feel the beggar but he told her "I have the dream to travel with magical drums and flutes" And he heard from her "I also want, I want your dream" So he told her "I will explain you my dream and how to make it reality" But she explained him "I want to do so many things in this world, right now I am focused on other things, all I know is that I don't want to live in routine" Then he asked her "So you want to be a child teacher?" He was still confused cause he had been told by Her prince that she was a doctor, so she explained him again "Yes I want to be a kids teacher" So he told her "I would like to hear you blow on your flute" She said "Wait a little here I go get my flute and I come back..."

The music beggar felt enchanted by The princess but he could not believe what was happening. He, even thought, she was not going to come back but he knew now that she was a fairy. He kept sitting in his convertible chair less than an hour when suddenly he felt from his back some strange feeling and turned his head and it was her with her yellow plastic flute that she did not like. She had in her hand also her note book with kid's melodies. She showed her flute to the music beggar and he right away said "I want to hear you make melodies" So she put herself one knee on the floor one knee on the air in front of him saying laying the melodies book on the floor of the street "You want to hear me blow on my flute?" And started blowing a child melody reading her book. When she had finished the music beggar enchanted said with deep peace and satisfaction "I love it..." She was pleased and smiled at him with so much satisfaction.

Then he wanted to try her flute and she accepted but he was not used to her flute, so he couldn't make nice sounds. She told him again that she wanted a wooden flute because she did not like this plastic flute...

The evening before The fairy princess had noticed when she passed by with a short skirt that he was sitting with another princess so she asked him "How is it going with your princess?" And he answered "Not much" as he did not care about that princess Ugne, so The fairy princess asked "Ah so she is not the one?" And he replied "No she is not, the one is another" And a strange thought crossed his mind #You are the one# The words did not come out of his throat but he pronounced them in his heart and in his mind. As The fairy princess could not see or hear words if they were not spoken she didn't hear his heart thought...Then after, they started a long conversation about the one Princess for his life...or the one Prince for her life. The fairy princess was all conversation long one knee on the floor one knee in the air and the enchanted beggar sitting on his convertible chair as he was always...

He told her that he never had a serious relationship with a princess because he was waiting to meet the real one for his life of whom he always dreamt about...He also told her that one magician had told him years ago that she will be taller than him and when he would meet her, he will then understand it was her...

Then he explained that when he would meet the one fairy princess for his life he would make her meet all his mother's family, and visit the house where he was born where he lived his early youth, where he dreamt about The fairy princess of his dreams. He also told her that he would want to bring her to a magical forest he knew in the north of a kingdom very close to the sea, and make melodies for the forest with her there, and also that he would want to travel with her to many other forests...Then The fairy princess told him "When I meet people, I know what I have to live with them" So quickly he asked her "So when you met your prince you knew it was The Prince of your dreams?" And she replied "No, he is not, he is just a prince with who I am living now..." So he became happy because that meant her prince was not her dream prince, but he remained very reserved and shy.

The fairy princess said "I don't care about coins" And the music beggar said "Yes coins are useless if we don't know how to use them, they just provide me for the tools I need, when I need something I pray to The king Jesus and because I look for the beauty in my mind and my heart, he makes me receive the coins I need" when suddenly, her plastic box started ringing, she stood up as if the music beggar didn't exist and talked to the plastic box, it was him, Her prince calling her.

The enchanted beggar felt and knew it was Her prince trying to get The fairy princess back to him. He was very sensitive and had visions of the truth and the real intentions of people...

When she finished talking with Her prince, she turned again her heart to the music beggar. He felt like he had to stand in front of what she will say even if it was against his heart and his dream. He felt, Her prince commended her to come help him and was shaking inside as his wish was going to be broken. And The princess told him "What's wrong?" He answered "I am so nervous now to speak with you" without revealing totally his thought and emotions to her. He knew he couldn't tell her that she had to stay right away with him and leave then with him the destined path they had together. And she asked "Why are you so nervous?" And he replied "Because I cannot be myself with you" And she said "Yes, you can, I am peaceful, I am like you, trust me" The music beggar became totally calm and started looking in to her eyes and she also started looking into his eyes. They were both in front of each other without moving and without talking, like in another dimension time... They were staring at each other and after while she said "You look so different when you are yourself"" And she added "Every spirit is so beautiful..." So he was fulfilled by inside joy because that meant to him that she thought he was beautiful for her...But he retorted "I don't agree, not all the spirits are beautiful" And hesitated to say, and finally said "You are the most beautiful spirit I have ever seen in my life..." The fairy princess smiled with an enormous satisfaction inside and said "That makes me feel very good about myself because I have many complexes..." The time again ad slowed down like the time did not exist anymore and the silence fulfilled their hearts. They were making with the breathing soft sounds of satisfaction and they were looking at each other with so much peace like nothing mattered anymore. The music beggar was then sure she was The fairy princess of his dreams, and felt they were going to be soon together. Because she told him that he could be himself, he started slowly to tell her what he really wished with silence between his statements..."I want to bring you to visit my mother's family...and I want to bring you to see the house where I was born...and I want to bring you to a magical forest I know, and I want to travel with you everywhere..." And she said looking in to his eyes..."I have to go, I have to help my prince and make dinner for him"

It was the beginning of afternoon and her prince had found the trick way to make her stop speaking to the music beggar...He knew then that she didn't feel his heart deeply and became oppressed by her words...He didn't know anymore what to say but he was sure that she did not feel his heart wishing that she would just leave right away with him, and she said "I don't want to leave you but, I have to" They kept looking at each other in peace. The music beggar had never felt this before and knew he had found what he was always looking for but, she said "We cannot look at each other like this for ever, life has to move" For him, it was all clear and it was not the right moment to break a so important heart meeting without space and without time, he felt like looking in to her eyes forever but he said "Alright" And she told him "I don't want to leave you but I have to..." After some silence he said "You have to help me because I don't want to let you go, it is too hard for me..." So she moved, turned her back walking away when he exclaimed out loud "Ah! That hurts so much! No, please stop" She made a step back to him and they looked at each other more time...But he knew that she would end up going to Her prince and he wanted to show her that he was strong so he said "Ok, I have to accept that you go now but I will not always accept that you leave me like this..." But they kept looking at each other as she remained still and was not leaving. He was totally still and could not move, he felt so much releasement and deep peace but she said again "I don't want to leave you but I have to..." And again she gave him her thoughts "Do you want to hug me before I leave?" He did not answer right away and kept looking in her eyes. The situation was slowing down. For him life was simple, she did not need to go make food for her prince because he was himself her real prince and he answered "I prefer not to, I am afraid it will be to short..." So she asked him again "So you don't want to hug me?" He kept looking in to her eyes so calmly. The time was slowing down and he was vulnerable in front of the situation, he knew he found what he was looking for and it was just going slide from his hands. His body was paralyzed, he couldn't move, he was so hurt, she was listening to the needs of Her prince instead of following his deep dream and he let his heart speak "Is not that I don't want to, it's that I prefer we wait..." So she asked again "So you don't want to hug me?" When his heart pronounced "I prefer to hug you when you will be ready for me, you are not ready yet..." His heart was like bleeding drops of sadness because he felt she was his love fairy princess but she was not ready for him and she had started her life with another prince. But she asked again "So you don't want to hug me?" Almost crying from the inside he answered "Of course I want to hug you... I want to hug you so much but I don't want to hug you and you leave me..." Silence fulfilled the moment...and space was empty, she asked then again "So you don't want to hug me?" And he opened totally his heart and said with tears in his words "I will give you more than a hug, I will give you all my heart, but when you will be ready for me, you are not yet ready" Without saying it, his mind, he felt ~it hurts me so much~ So she asked "You don't want to hug me because you will suffer after?" And he replied "Yes" with a very soft voice and a broken heart because she was joining Her prince...Then she told him "Ok I understand..."

Right before leaving, she said "I go now make dinner for my prince anyways we will meet again, you will turn your head and you will see me arriving" And he told her "Yes you know where I blow my flute" And she added "Yes, and you know where I live" Before she turned away, he told her looking deep in her eyes "I will be waiting for you..."

He watched her walking away. He noticed that she did not turn her head to look at him while walking away and felt he had lost something very precious. Like the clock had started a new beginning or a new end.

After that moment, he felt that they will be soon together as predestined and all bad thoughts disappeared. He somehow felt that talk was like a promise they will be soon *together but they accepted to let each other go each one their way until a reunion...*

CHAPTER 13
THE ENCHANTER'S NIGHT MARE STARTS

The same day in the evening, the music beggar was enchanting with his big magical drum. The fairy princess and Her prince passed by together holding hands, it made him feel dizzy and not good cause in his heart, he thought the situation was going to change. They just said "We are going to dance" and followed their way. He felt miserable and destroyed, after being so close to his fairy princess and seeing her with Her prince... He could not accept her passing by in front of him with Her prince anymore...

A few hours later he was still in the same place playing his plastic string tool under a porch protecting from the rain. The fairy princess and Her prince appeared again and stopped to speak with him. Her prince asked him "Are you alright, with the rain?" The music beggar did not care about the rain, Her prince had interrupted the most important moment of his life but he said "I love the rain and to sleep outside also" While they were speaking, The fairy princess started touching Her prince very gently with her soft hands. It was making dizzy the music beggar so he expressed it "I don't feel good" looking in her eyes...Her prince asked him "I worry for you, what are you going to do if it rains?" But the beggar didn't care to sleep on the streets, he cared about The fairy princess who was already so important to him. But they started speaking about music and Her prince asked her "So you are both going to play music together?" She answered "I cannot, I need to study" The beggar showed her a few written music ideas he made up, she listened to what he was explaining and then she took his plastic string tool and made sound a few chords. But after they left. The Enchanter felt destroyed...There wasn't anybody on the streets and some rain was falling so he went back to sleep under his crying trees. He could not sleep even one minute, the situation was hunting his mind and he stayed all night long feeling unwell inside.

Early in the morning, he went in front of her place enchanting the empty street with his flute while it was gently raining. After their run in their way home, The fairy princess and Her prince saw him, Her prince offered him a fruit and one tomato but he refused. He didn't want anything from Her prince, but Her prince didn't listen and left an apple and a banana in the bench besides him telling him before going to their living place with The fairy princess "I leave the fruits here for you if you want them" The music beggar did not need fruits but he needed to be with His fairy princess...Fruits could not fulfil his heart emotions instead of the company of His fairy princess.

Later he tried to go see His fairy princess at her balcony because he was so confused after that long talk they had the day before, but he only crossed Her prince. While waiting in front of her balcony, he wrote a poem for her explaining he needed her. They crossed each other later during the day, and his night mare started, every time he would see her with Her prince together he would feel dizzy. But that was not all, there was a suspicious crappy man smoking cigars who was coming every night invite him to sleep to his house saying that he was a god believer, but he felt he had bad intentions and saw in his heart that he was a black magic adept with real maniac intentions. And he saw true because one night late, when the streets was empty, while he was practicing his serenade plastic strings, that arrogant man appeared with a mask on his face holding a metal bar with his hand. The music beggar got scared at first but that man after took off the mask while laughing with so much arrogance. He just wanted to feel the pleasure to scare him.

The music beggar understood he had another enemy. He didn't fall in depressing because many nice young princesses were every day bringing him oho chips to feed him. He had somehow some support making him believe in his path...

One evening he was speaking to a woman when The fairy princess and Her prince passed by with new nice wheel tools, and they stopped to speak with him. He first spoke "I have to talk to both of you" And Her prince said with sureness "Well speak then" So he said "I need to speak to both of you separately" And Her prince said riding his wheel tool going away "Well then you will have to wait to meet us when we are not together" The fairy princess followed him to go to their living place and didn't stay to hear what the music beggar had to tell her.

One morning, while he was enchanting the street besides her living place, he felt some strange feeling from his back and suddenly The fairy princess passed by very fast with on wheel tool. Her prince was following her. The enchanting beggar wanted to speak to her but it was not possible she was going so fast. A few seconds after The fairy princess was riding fast, very fast towards him. His heart was beating strongly and he felt joy because he thought she was coming to speak with him and tell him she felt strong for him but he heard Her prince shout out loud "What are you doing!" He was following her.

But, she turned on a small street, and did not go to talk to the music beggar.

The day after The fairy princess and Her prince came to him again and The fairy princess told the music beggar "I saw you this morning in the akropolis" He felt, she wanted to speak to him and that she was attracted to him but Her prince said insisting to not let her speak with him "We have to go!" And she followed Her prince.

The music beggar had read the poems that he had written for her to an older woman he had met. That woman had told him that The fairy princess had to know his feelings. He thought the best was to be just be her friend because he thought she would not understand a music beggar living on the street could also love a princess living in the comfort, but that woman convinced him to tell all his heart feelings to The fairy princess...

A few days later the music beggar was in his usual place when The fairy princess and Her prince passed by and stopped to speak with him. Her prince announced him that he was going for one week in another kingdom for some free time for him. The music beggar felt that The fairy princess was going to stay and he will have time to speak alone with her.

Two days after he was enchanting with his flute and felt some soft feeling coming from his back making him loose control of his melodies. He turned his head to the left and The fairy princess was walking, fast she approached to him telling him "I don't have time to speak with you" He asked her "Will you stay while your prince is away?" She answered "Yes I will" So he said "Come see me, I need to tell you something" But she said "This week I am very occupied, I have too many things to do, I don't think I will have time" So he said "I just want to talk about something" And The fairy princess informed him "I don't think I will have time but I will maybe stop by..."

The fairy princess hadn't showed up for two days. When that morning he was wondering if she was going to appear suddenly while enchantment was coming out of his flute, a soft feeling coming from his left made him turn his head to the left, and there she was approaching and said "I don't have time to speak with you" He insisted telling her "It's very important, I need to tell you something" And she repeated herself "This week I don't have time to speak with you, I have lots of responsibilities" He persisted asking her "Did you tell me you liked my music projects?" She answered "Yes I do" So he told her "Come by, I need to talk to you about it..." She finally said "I will try maybe this afternoon"

CHAPTER 14
THE ENCHANTER TELLS THE FAIRY PRINCESS TO LEAVE WITH HIM

He was blowing on his flute all afternoon but The fairy princess did not appear. In the beginning of the evening when the sun was soon going to rest, he felt some soft feeling. He stopped blowing his flute, turned his head, and she was with her mother approaching him and told him "Wait, I will come in ten minutes" He had in paper written the three poems in the most famous language and the fourth poem he wrote in front of her balcony. He had the wooden flute he had bought for her and also the traverse flute that he also bought for her and also a bubble soap blower. He was going to express to her how he felt and give her the flutes.

Ten minutes after he was still in his place blowing on his flute and turned his head and saw her from one hundred walks approaching with her mother. She stopped to speak with him and her mother followed her way.

The fairy princess and the Enchanter of the flute were finally alone so he asked her "Did you tell me you also want my music projects?" ... "I don't remember what I said" she replied. He was confused so he asked again "Do you know how I feel for you?" ... "No I don't know" she answered.

So he handed to her the three poems and the fourth poem and told her "I wrote poems for you in the language you can understand, would you like to read them?" ..."Yes sure I want to read them" she said, grabbing the poems and put one knee on the floor and one on the air and read the them...

if you live the same dream as me
come with me and live it with me
going from forest to forests
nothing we will have missed

cause if our path is to be together
we have to leave like a feather
the wind will bring us to
our accomplishment
there will so much power at every moment

our creation will be from our inspiration
we will make together a same vibration
you don't want to live in routine
so just in my Life come in

like the bell of my life has rang inside of
my soul
and have to show you how strong I
fall in to your pole
you are written in my destiny to come
change everything
or rather to make my life like should
have been since the beginning

Now that I know that you exist
in my Life everything seems fixed
like if the clock had arrived to twelve and
it's the end
our dream today holds in to your hand

when you are in front of me I am like a
tree
we don't need to move to feel free
we will go everywhere and discover
between you and I will never be over

we will go to every mountain
our love will be like a never ending
fountain
your fingers will be moving for my
melodies and there will be fulfilment
I will hit on my drums to make your
flute sing the truth of our
Accomplishment

.

I am standing tomorrow with your flute
on my lips
yours were so still I felt them like an
eclipse
we will be in the full moons to change the
world
because for my ocean life you are the only
pearl
I don't need to cry cause I know together
we will go away
like two ducks down the river you are my
only way

looking at each other like in the same water
all what was before is not anymore a
matter
like the electrical lines we are aligned
I was brought here so you I can find
so many years feeling what I wanted to
become

there I am complete and tell all you
have to do is with me to come

When she had finished he asked her "Do you know now how I feel for you?" And she replied "Yes, you love me..." Then he told her "The word love is not enough to express how I feel for you" And explained her that she had to leave with him enchant the world with their kingdom melodies and handed to her an envelope with inside seven hundred coins in paper worth telling her "You did not get paid for your duties so the love gives you those coins you earned" But she told him "I cannot accept this paper worth coins from you, I wish that I would feel the same for you but I don't..." And he asked "So this means nothing for you?" And she replied "It means a lot but I have someone" Then he said "All right it means I am without sense..." She explained him how she thought..."You have your truth and I have my truth but I don't feel the same as you do" So he insisted "But you told me you wanted to travel" And she replied "Yes but I want to travel with my him and I love him so much..." Destroyed inside he said "I will leave your kingdom then, there is no sense I stay here..." So she told him "Yes go back to your kingdom and make your dream true alone making your melodies, we will to write letters to each other..." She gave him her address and added "Now I have to go I have lots of homework" Before she walked away he asked her "You said you wanted a wooden flute?" And she answered "Yes I do" So he took the box of the wooden flute and handed to her saying "Open it, it is for you"

She opened the box and saw the wooden flute, and she exclaimed "Wow" She was impressed. And he said "Try it" But she couldn't blow she never practiced on that flute before. So she said again "I will go now" And he said "Wait, I have this also for you" He handed to her the traverse flute. She took it with her hands but said "You should keep it" And he said "It doesn't make you happy?" She replied "Yes but you could keep it," So he asked "I bought it for you, so I give it to you, it doesn't mean anything for you?" And she answered "Yes it means a lot, it is for me a very precious gift. I am going now" And she then left, walking to her living place but when she arrived almost at the door, he called her by her name out loud. She turned and walked a few steps back to him, he also walked a few steps to her with the thirty three candles in his hands saying "I bought this candles to light with you on the roof of the abandoned building where I wanted to read for you your poems, but you have no time and you did not come, so you can light them with your prince" She said "You should keep them" So he told her "They will fall over my wheel carrier, have them please" So she accepted saying "All right, I take them, I have to go now" And then she left.

Two days after she passed by him saying again. "I don't have time to speak with you" The Enchanter had bought a pink very soft cover that he had forgotten to give her with the wooden flute and the traverse flute, so he told her "I forgot to give you this cover" And she said "I don't have space in my living place for this cover keep it" And she went away.

When Her prince came back one evening he passed by him, and music beggar asked him "Can you tell your princess I want to talk about my music to her?" But Her prince replied "No, she will go nowhere sorry" So the he said "I can speak to her just here" And Her prince told him "No she has to study" The music beggar knew studding was hard for her as she had told him so he told Her prince "Why wouldn't she make music?" But Her prince replied "She is too old for that, she had to start when she was twelve, if she wanted to do a music path. She likes children but she doesn't want to work or study. If she knew how hard is the career of architecture is, she wouldn't say her duties are hard"

The music beggar was preparing The fairy princess's music path and knew how easy music was but as The fairy princess would only listen to Her prince he could not do anything. He was very disappointed that The princess would choose Her prince and it was hard to enchant with his flute so he was singing like screaming his passion for her while hitting melodies of his magical drum.

CHAPTER 15
THE ENCHANTER BELIVES THE FAIRY PRINCESS WILL JOIN HIM SOON

That exact day was the one hundred years anniversary of her town. The town was full of music boxes blowing beats everywhere. He was changing his wet socks in to dry socks when The fairy princess and Her prince appeared and stopped in front of him. The fairy princess was dressed with a marvelous violet dress, and we could see the beautiful shape of her body making him feel crazy. He behaved very weird, so Her prince noticed it and asked him "What is wrong?" As the music beggar could not tell him what was wrong, he said with panic "I cannot blow my flute, don't you see there is from music boxes everywhere" Her prince handed to him one pear and for the only time the music beggar accepted the fruit grabbing it slowly because he was so charmed by The fairy princess's After Her prince took the hand of The fairy princess and went with her to their living place. The music beggar stayed just with the pear in his hand...

In the night when he arrived to his crying trees he was hungry and hadn't brought any food for him. He saw the pear somewhere in his wheel carrier and ate it. He felt like an invisible poison making him feel stressed out all night long like if his dream was becoming a night mare.

The day after was still the one hundred years celebration event and the music beggar was screaming singing his passion for her making poems with the words hitting his magical drum in front of her living place and they came to him but he ignored them and kept screaming. He preferred to scream passion poems for her than speak with Her prince. So they went their way. That evening he earned lots of coins, like lots more than one hundred and forty coins...

He had hard time accepting The fairy princess's rejection but wrote the first letter in the most famous language so she would be able to understand it. A few days passed and suddenly while he was blowing on his flute, he felt a soft feeling coming from his back and the control of his melodies slid, he turned his head and saw The fairy princess and asked to her "I wrote a letter for you, do you want it?" She answered "No I don't want it" And walked away.

The day after he was blowing his flute in a different place in the same street but, one hundred walks from his usual place when he feels a soft feeling coming from his back, he lost his melodies and turned his head and saw The fairy princess walking slowly like if she hadn't seen him. She was all dressed in pink, and she said "Ah...you are here..." He replied "Yes I am here" So she asked him "Do you have something to tell me?" And he answered "You don't want my first letter, so what else could I say?" So she replied with kindness "I did not say that I don't want your letter, I said I will take it when I will have something for you Ok?" And he replied with tenderness "Ok" And she walked away.

CHAPTER 16
THE ENCHANTER FINDS OUT
THE FAIRY PRINCESS LIKES HIM

A few days later he was playing his plastic string tool, when he felt a soft feeling from his back and fast turned, The fairy princess was approaching, she stopped on his left side and handed her letter to him saying "This is what I have for you, you can read it and if you have something to ask me, I will be back after buying my cracks and my fruits in the store" Her letter explained that he would not leave Her prince to go away with him...And at the end of the letter there was written #So you know it, I do love more dances than music #

The music beggar was then every sunny afternoon laying on the floor like a cow boy singing with his plastic strings tool, singing words for her, while she was living her life with Her prince.

That afternoon there was another princess from another kingdom besides him singing with him. They were having a talk when suddenly he felt a soft feeling so, he looked up, The fairy princess was walking slowly very close to the side where he was laying, he pronounced gently her name, but she kept walking slowly ignoring him as if she hadn't seen him so he called her by her name louder with more emotions asking "Is it you?" And she then turned to him saying "Yes it is me" And with lot of tenderness he said "Oh you look so different today" And she said "Oh, Thank you" So he asked "I have written the answer of your letter, do you want it?" She answered "Yes, I want it" He handed the letter to her. She put it fast in her food bag and walked away without saying a word. He watched her walk until she disappeared in the corner at the end of the street...With the letter he handed to her, he also gave his harmonica paper box with written in the inside #I do also love dances, but I reserve myself to dance with the fairy princess of my dream#

That day he was making up a music piece, he called it #You are like the moon# and the words were something like this...

You were walking slowly
With glasses hiding your eyes
I had to call you twice
Until you heard my voice
You accepted my letter
I watched you walk away
Until the end of the street
You are like the moon
Sometimes you give a little bit of your time
And I feel your love
Sometimes you totally disappear
And inside I feel the doubt
Only once I saw you full shining
And I felt your love
I am always siting like a lion
Waiting to shine on you again
And again I'll feel your love.

He was singing those words laying on the floor where he gave her his letter but for more than few weeks she was traveling with Her prince and did not appear.

One afternoon, while he was speaking to a very pretty princess two hundred walks away from his usual place just in front of the place where The fairy princess would always buy her fruits and cereal cracks, when he felt some strange waves coming from the left, he turned his head and The fairy princess was arriving. He could not speak anymore with the other princess with who he was speaking, because he felt without words, like out of mind control. The fairy princess made a sign to him waving her hand and entered in to buy her cereal cracks. And the other princess left because he couldn't speak after seeing The fairy princess pass by, so he was hitting his magical drum again when he felt a big wave inside and abruptly he stopped hitting his magical drum at exactly the same time as The fairy princess opened the door going out of the fruit store. She had rice cracks in her hand, she didn't look at him and walked back to her living place ignoring him.

Next day he was blowing his flute in the same place but showing his back to the place where The fairy princess would buy her fruits, when suddenly he felt again this big waves inside coming from his right side and stopped enchanting. He couldn't control his melodies and turned his head and there was The fairy princess approaching. He closed the eyes and breathed deeply and just felt...When a few seconds after, she appeared on his right side and asked him "How are you?" He was not all right but he answered "All right" She had painted three black dots under the left eye and three black dots under the right eye too. He felt threatened and said "I thought you did not like black dots on your face" And she replied "I changed my mind" It made him feel sad because he remembered her telling him that Her prince wanted her to paint her dots under her eyes in black instead of baby blue and she mentioned to him that she didn't like them in black. If she changed her mind it meant it was to please Her prince. Before going her way she told him that she was going to be away for the week end because she was going to dance with Her prince to another kingdom. Her birthday was during that weekend.

The next day the music beggar went to search for three eye pencils the same color The fairy princess drew the three blue dots under her eye, the day she came to speak with him in another dimension time offering him a lemon. He wrote in a blue paper the last poem he wrote for her that was a song called #You are the magical fairy# and packed the three pencils with the blue paper with that poem. That was going to be her birthday gift with another magical wooden flute he had ordered from another kingdom. He was wishing to see her and spend time with her but instead he was every afternoon standing crappy people sitting in front of him and people coming to annoy him, so he had to be strong and patient. . .

For one week The fairy princess had not passed by and more than two weeks he hadn't seen Her prince. That day he met a very pretty princess and was speaking to her in front of the food store. He was telling her his story with The fairy princess and accidently this princess was one of The fairy princess's friends, he was telling her "Your perfume smells not so good" when suddenly The fairy princess and Her prince were passing by and saw their friend talking to him so they went to speak to their friend. They ignored the music beggar while he was softly making romantic serenade melodies with his plastic string music tool, and then they went to buy their fruits. The other pretty princess went her way to watch the sun set. When the sun gave the darkness, she passed by again and stopped by him and he had the space to tell her "You are so not nice you abandoned me when I felt so bad" And this princess friend of The fairy princess said "I will give you a good advice never tell to a princess that she smells bad" So he told her "I never said you smelled bad, I said the perfume you put on you, smells too strong. I am sure you smell very good without perfume" They couldn't understand each other and she went her way.

After seeing his fairy princess holding the hand of Her prince, he felt so bad but so bad, that he left for the capital of her kingdom, the name of the capital was Vilnus. And he couldn't give to her the gift he had prepared for her.

CHAPTER 17
THE ENCHANTER LEAVES THE TOWN OF THE FAIRY PRINCESS TO THE CAPITAL OF HER KINGDOM

Once he was in the capital, he was looking for the place where he would blow his flute. One week after he sent a letter to The fairy princess to tell her that he left her town because she seemed to not want to speak anymore with him. But that was not exactly the reason, in fact he left because he could not live anymore seeing her all the time passing by holding hands with Her prince. She wrote him back that she did not feel guilty that he left her town because she did not ask him to...

Where he was making melodies with his plastic flute on his new place, a prince passed by him and told him "Your flute was blowing melodies so long time under my living place the other day" And he said "Oh yeah, I am always making melodies" That prince gave him a fifty coin paper for enchanting under his living place. He did not even remember that it was his birthday but he realized after. That same day The fairy princess received her magical wooden flute but she was away traveling with Her prince...So the parcel was delivered back to the magician woman in the kingdom where it was came from.

He wouldn't see anymore The fairy princess but they started writing letters to each other very often. There in his new place, one day he saw a princess crying because she had no place where to play her string music tool, he told her she could stay with him. And there she was coming every day to sit on the street besides him where he would make sound his flute and his harmonica. He was stopping many pretty princesses to speak with them, and all were very nice with him. He made also two friends a prince and a princess who were always in conflict, because they loved each other but, they were not, together, they were always in their shop checking nobody would steal the magical drums and also the magical wooden flutes.

CHAPTER 18
THE ENCHANTER OF THE FLUTE BECOMES THE ENCHANTER OF VILNUS GATVE AND WRITES MANY SONGS FOR THE FAIRY PRINCESS

. *Soon he started to blow his flute more time and found the place where he would enchant from midnight to three o'clock, in the street caring the name of the capital, Vilnus gatve. There he was enchanting every night for all the people of the kingdom passing by going or coming back from restaurants and bars to eat and drink, lot of them were throwing at his wicker basket many coins. And during the day he would blow his plastic flute and enchant the kids that would pass by him with their parents. The kids would stop in front of him looking in his eyes and his heart making him flow his joyful melodies for them. He became the Enchanter of Vilnus gatve. With all the coins he was receiving every day and* every night, he bought one accordion and one Spanish plastic string music tool he loved.

He wished somebody would capture his plastic string melodies to send to The fairy princess so she would come with her flute and let capture her melodies also to make music beauty together. And in front of the biggest prayer house he met a princess called Anna and her mother Renata introduced him to her father Ignas who had the power to capture music sounds because he had crophones and could stock the Enchanter's melodies in a plastic memorybox.

So Ignas started capturing all the melodies the Enchanter was dreaming of.

CHAPTER 19
THE ENCHANTER FINDS THE WHITE FEATHER DRESS

In kudirkas square The Enchanter wrote the first song in the capital in the most famous language, it was a sad poem for The fairy princess that he called -The Waltz of Vilnus- it was a simple waltz with only two chords but the sad poem had a dream melody that made him feel like that waltz was eternal, so he also called it The Eternal Waltz. It was the only music piece of his with words that The fairy princess had read, because he sent her the song words as a letter in the answer of words of hers telling to him that he was pessimistic on her opinion.

The poem's words were the answer to her opinion.

-The waltz of Vilnus-

I write words to check if you care or not care
life is so not fare
cause with me you don't want to play music
from not seeing you I feel sick

I ll be the man who will value you the most
you feel today my esteem for you is lost
I am the craziest musician in the earth
I ll make you realize how much you worth

rejected I feel sinking in the water
if just in my music you came playing
I would feel better
my life is amazing
but not perfect
cause with me you are not singing

and your beautiful soul I cannot protect
I have to hide for you what I am feeling

you take all the space in my heart
some words I tell you are not smart
you are like the sand
that I try to hold in my hand
with misunderstanding words
your mind flies like the birds
waiting for your answer
I should be tomorrow wiser

One afternoon he was walking around the capital Vilnus and he saw a white, so white dress with feathers on the shoulders and feathers on the hips, and imagined The fairy princess wearing that dress and went inside the shop and said "Please reserve this dress for me I will buy it for my fairy princess" But he thought that The fairy princess would think he was crazy to buy her a so expensive dress because she was already married to her prince, so he started buying other dresses and sending them to her in order to shock her with the white feather dress. He promised to her, that he will send her only 7 clothes but The fairy princess wrote him in a letter that she could buy herself her own clothes and that he did not know anyways what she liked. So he found a way to make her accept to receive dresses from him: He exactly wrote her "You say I don't know what you like, let's play this game, I send you clothes and you tell me if you like them or not" And she accepted that game. So he was spending all his coins in dresses for her. In total he spent more than one thousand coins earned blowing his little plastic flute on dresses for her before buying the white feather dress.

He was enchanting all the people of the kingdom every day and every night blowing his 7 coin plastic flute in the street Vilnus Gatve.

CHAPTER 20
THE ENCHANTER DANCES WITH THE FAIRY PRINCESS IN A DREAM AND HEARS THE TANGO OF PRAGUE

One night he had a dream where him and
The fairy princess were dancing on a flat roof
on a delightful music piece played by a music
box. It was a music piece with plastic string
rhythms and plastic string beauty melodies.
The dream ended with the music piece -The
waltz of Vilnus- In the morning he wrote her
a letter telling her the dream he had had but
she did not reply, she was traveling with Her
prince. He had dreamt they were dancing
magically together with eternal passion on
the roof of the highest abandoned building of
her town with melodies he had in his heart,
their love had been revealed... It was only a
dream, but the Enchanter of the flute knew
dreams could always become true if one would
trust on the magical power of the forces...so

he started following the dream, writing many music pieces for The fairy princess with soft dancing steps to make her dance as she loved to dance.

The fairy princess was not answering to all his letters because she was enjoying her life traveling with Her prince.

The Enchanter of the flute was also hitting his magical drum in kurdikas square for all the people passing by him and was writing music pieces for The fairy princess he wrote for her more than thirty three songs, but she had heard none of them because she was not going to visit him in the capital where he was writing them.

You all could think that his life was only amazing but it was not that easy because every night also in the capital he had to defend himself from not nice passengers who would want to take his coins earned and would tell him that this was not his kingdom saying he had to go away from there. People would also stop in front of him smoking paper burning in their mouth and he was allergic to that kind of smoke and that caused him lot of struggle, because lots of them did not want to leave the air free for him to breath and blow.

One day a crappy guy, took in front of the him his wheel tool caring his wheel carrier while he was enchanting Viluns Gatve so he had to fight because that crappy guy was determined to steal it from him and a young boy called Bazil helped him, and told him

"He is jalousie of you because you are talented, everything is going to be alright," and started crying from the injustice realizing the people around did not care, as he was musician, he understood what was to express the joy with melodies and be attacked, but a few minutes after two big guys friends of Bazil arrived and asked him what happened, and Bazil explained them, they ran up the long street looking for that crappy guy to teach him a lesson.

One evening a young prince, stopped to the Enchanter saying "I have a special coin look it is written Kuna, but I am not sure you are the right person to give to" the Enchanter told him "Don't doubt you have to feel" and that young prince said "Ok I feel yes I give it to you" In that coin there was scripted the shape of a ferret, his totem animal.

The Enchanter of the flute loved a place called svenciaus mergeles marijos ramintojos, it was a place looking like a house prayer where he wanted to make dance The fairy princess with his serenades but, as he did not manage to make her come see him, he could not make her wrists move and dance her gentle hips...

They wrote to each other many letters and he wrote many singing poems with music pieces for her and he bought for her many dresses until he found a little wooden music box. He was having the vision of The fairy princess reading to the kids the book he was writing, and he felt they were going to go around her kingdom read together the book of their story.

She had told him she was going to go visit him in the capital make melodies with him but instead she went with Her prince dance on an enormous gathering when a storm and an enormous wind was blowing in her whole kingdom. When she was back to her living place she sent him a letter telling him she was taking the bath with Her prince instead of writing him a nice letter, so the Enchanter sent her the little wooden little box and wrote her that she did not need Her prince in the bath cause she had the little wooden box to make melodies to her heart, and with Ignas the Enchanter wrote a music piece which he called #For her little wooden box on her ocean life#

He sent her one more beautiful dress. And The fairy princess wrote him that that was enough, that that was too many clothes not letting any free room in her closet. He then sent her a little paper box with which he wanted to make her proclaim the beauty of her heart melodies on his plastic string music pieces. . .

He warned her that there was still one last clothes arriving, but she answered #Enough is enough# So he explained her that it was too late, he already had bought it, so he went to buy the white feather dress, and sent it to her with a little metal white orchid to attach to her throat that was the symbol of her voice beauty. At first, she wrote him that she didn't like none of the dresses but after she thanked him for the white feather dress informing him that she liked it.

They were sending letters to each other and he was writing many music pieces for her. Sometimes she was not answering his letters and she was enjoying her life with Her prince Mindaugas traveling and dancing.

He was alone without The fairy princess of his dreams, but many other one princesses were bringing him food when he was hungry sitting on the floor with his flute.

CHAPTER 21
THE ENCHANTER HAS TO GO BACK TO THE TOWN OF THE FAIRY PRINCESS

The summer had arrived to its end, and it was getting colder, the leafs had fallen down. In the main street Vilnius gatve some wind had installed its self and not much people were passing by anymore, so the Enchanter was not receiving much coins so he started hitting the melodies from his magical drum on the biggest park of the capital, enchanting the kids during the afternoon when the sun was showing up.

One of those days, he decided to clean his bag, and he found a needle which was in his bag which he wanted to send to The fairy princess because she liked to sew. That needle was planted on the middle of the 8 number of the written 4,87 noted on a small piece of paper which was the price of the boxes he had to buy to send her all the dresses. He put it preciously inside of an envelope and sent it to her the day after. It was the sign of the magical love. Few minutes after a nice princess looking strong and confident passed by and stopped 7 walks from him. She opened her bag spreading pencils of all colors on the grass but she only took a normal grey pencil with a white paper and started drawing him.

Without understanding why, that day his magical drum was out of tune and only the builder who lived in the town where The fairy princess lived could tune it correctly because he was the builder of that magical drum and had the appropriate working tools for it, so the Enchanter had to plan to go there, it was

The fairy princess's home town, and agreed for a meeting with the magical drum builder.

One afternoon right before going to The fairy princess home town, in the way to the music shop tamsta walking by the beginning of the street uzupio the Enchanter of the flute saw on a garbage bin a long and wide coat of his favorite color, blue green dark turquois. He picked it up and went to clean it in the river, and knew it was the magi of the power forces offering him a coat of the color he liked most. He knew he will wear that coat during the winter

Strangely the Enchanter was dreaming of buying a harp for The fairy princess, when at the same time, The fairy princess sent him a letter telling him that she liked the little paper and wooden boxes, the magical drums and also the arfa sounds that is how she called the harp in her language. In her letter it was written "Now you know what I like" Anyways The fairy princess didn't need to tell him, because he already had sent a letter to the arfa builder ordering one for her, as he would see her dreams before she dreamt them and made everything to make them true.

The Enchanter sent her a letter warning her that he was going back to her town and they could meet and that he was bringing his new magical big moon drum and he could lend it to her so she could make melodies for the kids, but she replied to him that she did not want to see him or receive music tools from him because she was loved by him and that was not good. It was like this "I am coming back to your town to tune my magical drum we could meet and make our heart melodies" and The fairy princess thoughts "I don't want to see you and I don't want you to buy me more music tools because you love me"

When he arrived to her living town he was wearing a white shirt looking like a prince and he was full of music tools, and had black garbage bags in and on his wheel carrier full of his new elegant clothes to dance with her. On his back bag, he had the new big moon drum he brought because he knew The fairy princess wanted one for her kid's sleep time. And when he was riding his wheel tool to the meeting with the magical drum builder, The fairy princess saw him passing by riding with his wheel tool and she sent him a fast letter informing him that she saw him from her kid's school window. The Enchanter gave the magical drum to the steel drum builder and went after to check his fast letter box and read The fairy princess's letter "Actually I just saw you passing by my kids school" He became so happy and excited and joy was in his heart.

The Enchanter then knew where The fairy princess was keeping and taking care of the kids of her kingdom because there was only one school in the way he rode his wheel tool. His deduction made him understand it. He wanted to go see her teach the kids and bring her the big magical moon drum so she could make sleep the kids but, The fairy princess was busy and did not answer. She replied later like this "We will meet, if it's meant to be"

CHAPTER 22
THE ENCHANTER AND THE FAIRY PRINCESS MEET IN AKROPOLIS AFTER MANY MONTHS APART

The day after The fairy princess was going to the beach dance with Her prince and the Enchanter stayed without meeting her. But few days later, when he was in his way to buy a bottle of water in akropolis because he was very thirsty he saw, The fairy princess sitting on a table speaking to her plastic box eating a chocolate cake. He went to buy water as he was so thirsty and then sat behind her. When she had finished talking to her plastic box he called her asking her "May I join you?" She accepted saying "But not for a long time because I need to write my mind stories on my blue notebook" The Enchanter was very nervous, he hadn't seen her for more than four months. He spilled water on himself while drinking and talking at the same time.

The fairy princess explained him "Work with kids is very hard...They don't want to learn and they don't want to sing with me the song I wrote for them" The Enchanter knew that kids felt when a princess was not honest to herself and they wouldn't want to hear what that princess would say or commend, because kids loved sweet, spontaneous and nice honest behavior like butter flies. They knew it was useless to be strict if life was meant to be easy...The kids felt she was not in her real life but besides her life looping from one side to another side of her real path...The kids simply felt the truth of life...

The fairy princess was very kind and soft with him. She had joy and happiness to look in his eyes but her plastic box was making sounds and she said "I am going to have to talk with my plastic box it will connect me to my mother's thoughts" So the Enchanter asked if he should leave her alone and she told him that the talking box moment would last long so it was better for her to be alone, so he left and went to enchant in front of her living place, where they had had the moment in another dimension time and while he was putting his pink coin box in front of him, an autumn leaf with two pink petals attached to the leaf stick laid on the box moved with gentleness by a soft blow of wind...It was four o'clock, a dark afternoon of autumn, but the pink petals were visible and totally alive. He took that magical leaf by his hand and got fulfilled by a gentle feeling. He put it in an envelope and stayed amazed by The fairy princess's small magi.

The Enchanter was blowing melodies every afternoon starting from four o'clock when the sun was sat and the dark was showing up to inspire his heart, because he didn't like the cloudy sky but loved the dark star sky.

The first time he saw The fairy princess passing by she was dressed with a pink coat and said to him "I don't have time because I am late for my gymnastic dance classes"

The second time she was wearing the baby blue rain coat that he bought for her for 99 coins and that made him joyful but she did not either look at him either spoke at him.

The next day The fairy princess sent him
a letter telling him that he could join her at
Her prince's office late at night where she
would be studding alone and that he could
take his tronic steel string tool that Her
prince was keeping and his other music tools
too, but the Enchanter had so many tools and
clothes to carry around, so he answered to
her letter that she could come pick him up
in his under road transition after nine o'clock
where he would be waiting for her...But The
fairy princess did not go and when he had
finished enchanting after midnight he passed
by Her prince's office work and there was no
light on, so he deduced she was not there and
went to sleep.

During that month, he was blowing on his silver elegant music tool and he wrote a music piece that he called # If love is above #

There's no more to say
You know how I am crazy
Ridiculous I am singing like a dear
Without shame for you I am
standing without fear

With you I'm without any success
I don't think of you like a toy sex
Around this desire I am above
With you is all about Love

I first saw you in pink
You told me to never think
Second I saw you in blue
I was stock on the ground like with glue

I try to open your hearts door
You such of woman hard core
You put my head down on the floor
Feel down but want some more

Like a lion want to sit on the sun
Want to feel you are my
mother and I am your son
Want to sit all in peace
All your damages just release...

Don't be looking for yourself
Just find out you are my real elf

CHAPTER 23
THE ENCHANTER LOOKS FOR A WAY
THE FAIRY PRINCESS WILL ACCEPT
HIS LOVE

Days were passing by and The Enchanter of the flute was sending letters to The fairy princess insisting that he could come bring the magical moon drum to her, but The fairy princess didn't want to have things from him because she felt she belonged to Her prince so the Enchanter found an idea, this idea was to tell her that he needed help because he had too many bags and too many music tools to carry around on his wheel carrier and it was too heavy and that the keepers in the big buying store place were complaining for keeping every day his big moon drum which anyways all was true and not a lie, it was just to convince her because he knew she wanted to have his magical big moon drum. She finally accepted to help him, but she didn't want to give him the exact day or the exact time she would come take the moon drum and meet him so in order to get an exact day he explained her in a letter that he had to go see his brother to help him so he needed to organize his trip and leave the moon drum to her soon because it would be too many things to carry in his way crossing the few kingdoms he had to cross.

They finally agreed to meet the evening of seventh November. The evening before the Enchanter wrote a special waltz for The fairy princess #You are like a Rose# it was a waltz in his kingdom language in five step feet. That evening his plastic strings tool fell on the floor and nocked the neck mechanics, so he couldn't tune the plastic thinnest string.

A special magical tuning was condemned by the twisted mechanics, and he understood it was the power of the invisible forces that were making magi happen. He found harp chords for The fairy princess and he called those chords the Shaman Girl...

CHAPTER 24

THE ENCHANTER AND THE FAIRY PRINCESS PLAY MUSIC TOGETHER FOR THE FIRST TIME

When The fairy princess arrived to the meeting on the seventh November, she was acting distant and shy, so like a gentleman the Enchanter told her "Sit in this chair please" He had prepared the chair for her it was one of his boxes. The fairy princess had brought her little wooden box and her little paper box to express her melodies to him so they could share their heart melodies making sounds for each other. And after then the Enchanter took his plastic string tool with the condemned tuning and sang some words for her while she made sound his magical moon drum...He was singing to her in a romantic language she could not understand... He was loving that delightful moment but he was a stressed out and worried because to be with

The fairy princess meant that Her prince could appear at any moment to interrupt their melodies and bring her to his living place or call her by her plastic box and make her go home like he had done before showing that she was His...A boy was passing by. He had a magical moon drum and interrupted them asking if he could play with them but the Enchanter wished since so long to be alone with her and was waiting all those long days and months to make melodies with her alone, so he made a sign to that boy that it was not possible. When they stopped making melodies she asked him "Is it like that how you treat people who are friendly with you?" Without hesitating, he answered "Melodies should never be interrupted when they are sent from the heart"

After a little time, she said that she was cold, so fast the Enchanter started packing his heavy big magical moon drum but it cost him concentration to zip the bag with the big moon drum in because he just wanted to stay with her instead of letting her go. When he managed finally to fit it in the bag and zit it, he handed it to her as the agreement was made, so she could go safely fast inside her worm living place. He felt unsatisfied because they didn't go together to a worm place drink something but that was how it happened...

Few days later, the Enchanter left for a long trip to see his brother caring his big elegant music tool, sleeping bags, his plastic string tool in his back and more bags...There he visited his friend who had psychic abilities who told him many things about The fairy princess which was revealed to him by the power of the invisible forces. The Enchanter then knew...The fairy princess was testing him, and she enjoyed creating emotions inside of him...But he needed a kind fairy princess not a princess who played with his feelings and made him experience jalousie, he was just a simple person.

When he was with his brother, he received a letter from her where she explained that she did not want to make melodies with him anymore because she felt not comfortable around him, and that she wanted only to write each other, one letter a year or just a few but not so many...So he stopped writing her, and he wrote in the living room of his brother a song called "You are my Muse" it was the last song he wrote for her in the most famous language at that time.

During the time he spend there he worked hard making holes in the yard of his old good friend, so he could pay with the coins earned the arfa he ordered for The fairy princess cause he knew that The fairy princess really wanted an arfa, even if she wrote him that she didn't want anything from him anymore.

When he had worked enough to pay the arfa, he said good bay to the donkeys in front of his brother's, and sent all those coins to the arfa builder so the arfa would be sent to the place where The fairy princess kept the kids and taught them things she had to. Then he left back to The fairy princess's kingdom...

The fairy princess had told him by a letter that she didn't want to receive anything from him anymore at her living place, but he knew her kid's teaching school place address, and he did ask to the harp builder to send it to the school so she would receive it there... And he sent her another letter asking her if she could keep another new magical drum he had bought, to which she answered "I will keep it, only if you help my prince have one

for us, we want your magical space drum, it
sounds very good when you hit on it,"

CHAPTER 25
THE ENCHANTER FINDS ON HIS PLASTIC STRING TOOL HIS MASTER PIECE THE TANGO OF PRAGUE

In his way back, he was caring with him so many things, two sleeping bags and one cover to sleep outside his elegant music tool and his plastic string tool on his back and arrived with all those weights to a kingdom called Prague where the guards told him he had to pay one thousand coins to the kingdom because he was playing three minutes too late that was not allowed in their kingdom. Before leaving Prague he found dancing sounds with his plastic string tool to make dance The fairy princess, they were like the rhythmic chords he heard in the dream he had where they were him and the fairy princess both dancing eternally together on the roof of an abandoned building. Those sounds he heard in the dream had no singing voice, it was plastic strings rhythm chords rolling on time and on them laying a simple melody. As he was in Prague he called that piece #The tango of Prague# It was like he had dreamt this music piece but only found them in his plastic string tool after which was now in the true real story. The past and the present became one, still was left the future to dance with her on the music piece...

After, he crossed another kingdom called Krakovia where the guards of that kingdom told him to not blow his flute and threatened him with a gas spray but a group of nice boys helped him to scape that danger. That was very close to The fairy princess's kingdom. He tried to get inside big power machines, but he had trouble because in that kingdom they didn't like different people and he looked very strange so full of music tools and covers but he managed to cross that kingdom.

When he arrived to The fairy princess's town, he started enchanting with his flute. Not many people were giving him coins and he had the wish to buy for himself a silver trumpet. But soon was the end of the year and lot of people were out walking on the snow and his harmonica dancing with him blowing happy melodies were making the passengers feel the joy of the end of the year and he was receiving many coins...For the end of the year, he wanted to buy a pen for The fairy princess, the same color of her note book of the color shining blue because he knew she liked to write her thoughts in that note book but he forced himself not to buy it because she did not understand that he would spend all his coins on her.

CHAPTER 26
THE ENCHANTER WANTS TO
BUY A LITTLE CASTLE FOR
THE FAIRY PRINCESS

The Enchanter knew the winter was soon arriving and asked The fairy princess if she would help him find a living place cause he did not speak the language of her kingdom. "Fairy princess would you help me find a little living place where I could sleep that I could buy?" But The fairy princess told him to ask to Her prince "Enchanter you should ask to Mindaugas he knows the kingdom laws better than me" But the Enchanter didn't feel good around him, so he tried to explain to her that Her prince and him had not easy mutual understanding. She finally agreed to help him after he explained her many times, so she organized a meeting with the owner of half of one house one day with no exact time, but he missed that meeting because there was no exact time agreed. He had to cross many fields, and many roads with his wheel tool. He arrived and saw nobody there and thought nobody would come to meet him and left.

Then The fairy princess wrote him "You are not nice to people, that gentleman has done three hundred thousand walks with his wheel machine to meet you and you weren't there" Then he replied to her letter "I also made lots of walks sweating rolling my wheel tool to arrive there" But she didn't want to hear and wrote him "Find it yourself, I won't help you anymore" After he wrote her that he found a little castle that he really liked, where she could put all the dresses he had bought for her because she complained that she had not enough space in Her prince's living place, but she did not want to visit that little castle and did not take him seriously and wrote him "You want me to buy you a little castle so you can live there, hah I don't work, Mindaugas provides everything for me so I can't buy it for you sorry that's what you want to, play games?" She didn't believe him when he announced her that he had received a bag of many coins from his family because the invisible forces were making every step of his mission dream true in his real life...

So she didn't believe he wanted to buy that little castle for her and mocked him with her irony. He told her then to not tell Her prince that he wanted to buy a little castle for her but she did tell Her prince any ways...

CHAPTER 27
THE ENCHANTER MAKES WITH HIS FLUTE DANCE THE FAIRY PRINCESS

It had been long time since the Enchanter hadn't crossed The fairy princess' prince but he appeared there to his under road transition and invited him to have dinner with them. He didn't feel to go to his invitation because as soon as he saw Her prince coming to him, he felt tension like heavy lead in his heart, but he accepted because he knew he needed to see her as his psychic friend told him.

When he entered in their living room, he saw her working on her kids writing lessons and they did not look at each other. The fairy princess had told him that she did not want to make music or see him anymore, so it was strange to be brought there at her living place. He did not know how to act so he sat down on the floor silently because the table was on the floor and gave attention to Her prince's music lead box, and slightly glanced at her sometimes. Every single time he had to speak to Her prince, he felt tension in his heart because he could not tell him what he really felt. He tried to answer to all his questions politely and waited that the food was ready. Her prince was asking him many questions, until the other princess guest arrived and spoke with them also. The Enchanter then noticed the flute that he sent to The fairy princess was hanging on her blue steel string tool and asked her if he could blow on it. She answered that he could, so he tried her flute. And then he asked her if he could play her string tool, he wanted to try the string sounds of the Shaman girl chords while her blowing in to her magical flute. She grabbed her magical flute and blew on it her heart child melody. The Enchanter loved it, he felt so joyful and pleased that some strange low sounds came out of his throat expressing his inside joy. Then Her prince said to all, it was time to have dinner so they started eating. The Enchanter's appetite was cut. Her prince wouldn't let him time to look at The fairy princess and was asking him many questions and talking to him without rest so he didn't eat much.

A bad news were going to be told, it was Her prince telling the Enchanter. "With my princess we are going to celebrate New Year in Prague" That was where the Enchanter of the flute had found the chords of The tango of Prague to make dance The fairy princess, so he felt unhappiness but didn't say it...

When they had finished eating they started to make sounds with all the music tools that the Enchanter of the flute had bought for The fairy princess. He was very attentive to The fairy princess's moves and feelings and was trying to offer her the little paper box so she would make her peace kingdom melodies and he could feel her heart beauty but, Her prince would put his lead music box loud and would destroy her finger melodies' softness making the Enchanter unsatisfied so with his throat he started making some ancient low sounds to be louder than Her prince's music box. The fairy princess was closing her eyes like when she first saw him hitting his magical drum. He felt she was there together in his peace sound garden alone with him both alone the two of them together dreaming...like in another dimension time again...

The end of the meeting almost arrived. Her prince asked the Enchanter to blow on his trumpet but the Enchanter was very sensitive and felt he had to take his plastic flute and said "I need my flute that is in my bag" The fairy princess stood up fast, trying to grab his flute from his bag but the other princess guest was closer to his bag so she took it first and handed to him and he started blowing on his plastic flute enchanting The fairy princess while Her prince's lead music box playing. She stood up and right away started dancing on his flute enchantment. He was so fulfilled with joy feeling an enormous satisfaction...He was on the floor laying. He was getting closer and closer to her because he was moving to give himself space from the table annoying one of his arms. Moving like a worm he was trying to put himself in a place where space was...

But right before they got too close, Her prince stopped his music box and straight away after, the guest went to the door to leave the place. Her prince joined her to open the door and The fairy princess found herself in front of the Enchanter, in front of the music Prince who was waiting that she will leave with him. She stood up escaping the situation avoiding his heart, and went fast to stand beside Her prince. After the guest, Her prince and The fairy princess hugged a three person hug. The Enchanter of the flute felt unsatisfied alone sitting still on the floor, so he decided to leave, and stood up. When he walked to the hall where the door was to get ready to put on his blue green coat, there The fairy princess slid fast herself in front of him moving her hands between his coat that was on the floor and him standing. He could not get his long blue green coat, she was there in the middle moving sensually her hands and her wrists as for the beginning of a dancing serenade. He was looking at her fulfilled by peace, feeling her wrists hand moves. She was moving her wrists and her hands with love looking at him as if she was still dancing for him and was ready to leave with him. But, Her prince fast told the Enchanter out loud with his aggressive voice "Now you have to go!" When fast she stepped on the side of Her prince as if he owned her letting the Enchanter take his long blue green coat. The fairy princess would do everything to please Her prince and would not read his heart

feeling so hurt. Then she handed her hand
to him, he shook her hand politely and Her
prince handed to him a peach. He guessed
that it was The fairy princess who had told
him what fruit he liked because she knew
his taste. Losing his dream for Her prince's
pride glory could not be consoled by anything
in this earth...

CHAPTER 28
THE ENCHANTER STARTS LIVING IN HIS ABONDON PALACE

When he went outside it was very cold, it was beginning of winter, to his mind came the idea to go sleep in the abandon building where he wanted to bring and read the poems in his language to The fairy princess. When he arrived at the building, he attached his wheel tool with a weak locker and walked all the stairs up caring his sleeping tools to sleep on the top floor. In the middle of the night he heard boys shouting screaming very loud. In the morning his wheel tool was no longer there. He had been stolen his carrier and his wheel tool.

The Enchanter had forgotten his gloves in The fairy princess's living place. Enchanting with his flute outside in the middle of winter was very cold for his fingers but he didn't know he forgot them in her living place but she saw them laying on the floor of her living room so she brought the gloves to him when he announced her that he got stolen his wheel tool and his tool carrier "Please don't be cruel to me I have been stolen my tool carrier" And The fairy princess got worried "So they took all your music tools?" And he reassured her "They only took the wheel carrier and the wheel tool with nothing inside"

The fairy princess was optimistic "Don't worry it will appear, they were just playing"

She handed him his gloves and he asked her if she could repair his hat "Can you make me a favor?" And she said "It depends what"

So he asked "You, who likes sewing, would you sew my Russian hat for me? The button is broken" She refused saying "Ask somebody else, look this ballerina I painted it, today it is my first paint class" showing to him her painting before she went to her living place.

In the evening the Enchanter was blowing melodies out of his trumpet and The fairy princess passed by and she said "I am going for a walk" In her way back, she stopped and told him "I saw your wheel carrier close to the river" He went where she said it was and found there also his wheel tool. Then he went back to blow his flute in the cold underground Transition until he was tired and went to sleep in his abandoned palace.

Few days later, he asked her on a letter if she could bring him the heart drum plastic sticks. In the evening she brought them to him as he had asked her and she told him "I don't want you to use my living place to stock your music tools or to receive them, is that clear?" There was another princess dressed in a beautiful short dress waiting she finished speaking to him but The fairy princess was so long speaking to the Enchanter that, that other princess left and never showed up again. The Enchanter asked The fairy princess "So you want me to give my magical heart drum to your prince so you can blow your melodies for him?" And she answered "I don't know he wants it for himself" So he then said "Ok tell him to come I will have it in two days" And then she left.

CHAPTER 29
THE ENCHANTER LENDS HIS MAGICAL DRUM TO THE FAIRY PRINCESS' PRINCE

When he had back his magical drum, Her prince came to take it, and the Enchanter of the flute asked him "I have a project for The fairy princess where she can blow on her flute where her melodies can be captured and it would make possible for other to listen to her melodies in a plastic round shining circle so every people in the world will be able to have it in their living places and will be able to listen to her heart melodies, without her and I being with the plastic circle at the same time"

The Enchanter of the flute had many ideas for his music pieces where The fairy princess could play her little wooden box, her little paper box with also her magical wooden flute making soft melodies from her heart kingdom.

He had written many music pieces for that project called #the peace of the anchanter of the flute# but Her prince said "She is an amateur, she needs to practice she is in to dancing, I know another princess who plays very good music, she has the same name as my princess but she plays all type of music tools. She is in another kingdom right in this moment, one day I will make you meet her" The Enchanter of the flute did not care about Her prince's friend princess who played well music tools and was called the same name as The fairy princess, he only wanted to share his melodies with The fairy princess but he said "Ok, ok" He knew it was useless to try to explain anything him. The Enchanter felt frustrated but let Her prince leave with his magical drum.

In his abandoned palace, after blowing his on the cold, The Enchanter of the flute was playing romantic serenades with his plastic string tool. As his dream had delivered to him in his dream by the higher forces, he found there on the top of his palace the beauty plastic string melodies that would be laying on the rhythm chords he had found in Prague as resonated in the dream offering his tango passion to the accomplishment of his master piece #The tango of Prague# to dance with The fairy princess on the flat roof of his huge abandoned palace.

Before the end of the year instead of going to find the Enchanter, The fairy princess wrote him a letter saying "We can meet, if you want, for one hour this afternoon at one or two or three o'clock" The Enchanter didn't know but, The fairy princess had bought gifts for him, but he read the letter too late and when he answered The fairy princess was busy preparing the Christmas tree in the living place of Her prince's parents, and it was too late.

CHAPTER 30
THE ENCHANTER OF THE FLUTE
SEES THE FAIRY PRINCESS DANCE
FOR HER PRINCE

The fairy princess sent him another letter "I have no time to meet you but my prince wants to invite you to a gathering and we will make sounds and melodies there" In the evening The fairy princess and Her prince explained to him where the gathering was happening and they joined each other there.

They were bringing all the music tools the Enchanter had bought for The fairy princess with their wheel machine. They arrived first and waited for the Enchanter, when he was in front of them The fairy princess handed the gifts to him with kindness saying "This are the gifts I bought for you" Her prince took out all the music tools from his wheel machine and handed a few of them to The fairy princess and put the others on the

Enchanter's music tool carrier. Then they entered in the main hall and walked the stairs up to the gathering. He was feeling uncomfortable, because he was acting like a simple friend to The fairy princess. As soon as they arrived in front of the entrance door, The fairy princess positioned herself besides the Enchanter and they entered together as if they were in love. She took away her coat in front of him like with a seduction purpose, like to impress him. She had on a black dress with a long cut on the left and the right side, starting from the feet until the edge of the hips showing her entire legs when she would move her legs or dance.

Then they both entered in the main room also together one besides each other as if they were in couple. The guests were talking to each other or drinking wine. The Enchanter was trying not to speak with her because he was trying to hide how he could his feelings. They once crossed one another exchanging a few words but Her prince came interrupt them right away offering her a glass of white wine that she accepted taking it with her hand and drank the wine in front of the Enchanter. He was trying not to offer her his attention pretending he was just a casual friend with normal interest towards her. He should have hit on his magical earlier but he was hesitating. Finally he grabbed his drum and started hitting melodies out of it. He did not expected it at all but Her prince took The fairy princess by her hand making looping her body and started to make her dance on his magical drum's melodies...

He was not feeling good inside. To see His fairy princess dancing for Her prince on his hitting sounds was heavy on his loving heart, but he made it seem like it did not affect him and kept hitting the drum pretending he was strong, until The fairy princess and Her prince got tired of dancing together. The Enchanter was still hitting sounds with his magical drum and The fairy princess was sitting on the floor besides her moon drum and was making her peace melodies hitting the metal petals of her little moon drum beauty with her soft fluffy ball sticks. The Enchanter was pleased and was hitting softer to be able to hear her soft melodies, but a gentleman started speaking out loud on the top of his and The fairy princess's melodies. The fairy princess's prince went fast besides the Enchanter's left side and stopped with his hand the Enchanter's hands from hitting melodies with The fairy princess. She then found herself hitting softly her melodies alone on the speech of that gentle man.

Some of them spoke each one their turn trying to prove to each other they knew better than other what the one in the middle of the circle pretended to imitate. The Enchanter saw The fairy princess back laying on the wall and wanted to go sit be sides her but there he saw Her prince sit before him so he didn't go and stayed unsatisfied. He then was standing and Her prince made a sign to him to express he had to sit like everyone in the room but the Enchanter got bored very fast so he crossed the room trying nobody would notice him and was ready to leave the place, but when he arrived to the kitchen where he was drinking water to satiate before leaving the place, Her prince came in to the kitchen and asked him "Why are you leaving?" He replied "I just need to enchant outside, I want to buy a new iron trumpet for myself" But in fact he wanted to leave because he couldn't stand to be away from The fairy princess and see her with Her prince...Her prince told him "It is not good in Christmas time to be alone" The Enchanter preferred being totally alone than seeing The fairy princess dancing holding the hands of Her prince. Again Her prince made pressure to him so he would stay at the gathering. The Enchanter trying to find an acceptable reason to be able to leave was explaining that he needed to earn more coins in order to buy material to make his hand made shoes with goat fur to be worn in his cold palace when another gentleman came in to the kitchen getting involved in the conversation. He wanted to know more about the winter shoes he was planning to make, The Enchanter got distracted and told to that gentlemen about the sandals he made of the heart shape and mice ears. They walked together to the dancing room speaking some more.

When they had finished their talk, the Enchanter saw The fairy princess sat close to her little moon drum playing with a little kid. He took her little paper box laying somewhere close to her and handed it to her, but she put it on her back and avoided his eyes and his attention. Then he went alone to the hall and opened up one of the two gifts he had been given by The fairy princess. It was a bracelet in the same shape as his tronic string tool, he put it on his ankle instead of his wrist. he had to put oil all the time on his hands to prepare them for the cold air of the winter before playing his cold flute so he needed his wrist free. After he went to ask The fairy princess who was still playing with the little kid "Can I open my other gift?" She accepted "Yes you can" So he went to the hall again where he left them and put himself one knee on the floor one knee on the air and started opening the other gifts when fast The fairy princess joined him and put herself one knee on the floor one knee on the air telling him "You can only open them if you have found the small bracelet tronic music tool first" He said "I have, I am wearing it" She couldn't see the bracelet on his wrist "But I don't see it on your wrist" And he answered showing to her his ankle "Because it's here, I don't put it on my wrist because many times in the day I need to put oil on my hands and make an eight exercise to prepare them for the cold outside when I blow my flute and I have to take care of my dreaming hands for the dancing shows that I prepare for the princess Evelina...I only have talent, gift in my hands and have to take care of them" He was explaining to her that Evelina cried in front of him and that it touched his heart, when suddenly some guests entered in the hall, and The fairy princess fast told the Enchanter "Let's go to the kitchen, there is no body there" So they went to the kitchen where fast she took a glass poured water from the tab and drinking quickly in panic asked him "So what were you telling me?" It took some time for him to remember but he finally answered "Oh, about my hands yeah, I need to take care of them yes" And her almost cutting his words said immediately "You were telling me you found another princess your gifted fingers will make dance in shows for the people of my kingdom?" And he said the truth "Yes, she cried in front of me and it touched my heart" And abruptly The fairy princess said "I want to dance now" And left right away the kitchen by herself and went walking fast in to the small dancing room. The Enchanter was astonished and went in to the living room and saw from there that she was dancing on her own and Her prince besides on his own too. He tried to not go with them but some power forces brought him there without him being able to control it. So in that same room they found out the three of them dancing on their own, The Enchanter Her prince and The fairy princess.

The Enchanter danced almost jumping to the ceiling the same way he was dancing on the snow for all the people of her town when blowing his harmonica. The fairy princess was moving her wrists as if she was dancing a spanish romance dance but, like sending her inside beauty to the window instead of to him. When the music box had finished some guests were leaving the gathering. Her prince went to the hall to bid them because he knew every one of them. The fairy princess went to his arms to show she was His. The fairy princess was kissed by Her prince and the Enchanter saw it and felt dizzy and lost. A few seconds after Her prince took her again by her hands making her loop on the sounds of the man hitting the Enchanter's magical drum. The gentle man owner of the place where was this gathering grabbed the Enchanter's plastic string tool and handed it to a very pretty princess who was sitting on the right side of the couch of the big living room and that pretty princess started making the plastic strings sound. The Enchanter felt lost seeing The fairy princess again dance by Her prince moves, so he grabbed the bamboo flute he had bought for her and started blowing but the sounds were not clear. He hadn't practiced much with that flute before sending it to her, he couldn't blow on it properly. Then he wanted to make the sounds become louder as that was the reason he was born and started to blow the bamboo flute sounds towards the hole of his plastic string tool laying on the other pretty princess's thighs to amplify the flute sounds. He was so unpleased, The fairy princess and

Her prince were again dancing together...he did not know what to do, So he kept blowing to the bamboo flute down on his knees in front of the pretty princess making sounds with his plastic string tool. He was trying to distract himself and not watch The fairy princess and Her prince dance. He was blowing her bamboo flute inside his plastic string tool still on the pretty princess's thigh, and some power invisible forces made him stand and dance in circle blowing the sounds out of the bamboo flute around them dancing. Back and forth he was dancing and putting himself on his knees in front of the other pretty princess to blow the sounds of the flute on the hole of his plastic string tool. Suddenly while he was standing some powerful low ancient sounds came out of his throat, like in a very old way of speaking words blowing towards The fairy princess and Her prince, he was no longer dancing around them...He was then switching from being on his knees blowing her bamboo flute on the hole of his plastic string tool on the thigh of the other pretty princess and after standing making those strange old chanting without moving. He was trying to not look at them to not suffer closing the eyes and opening every few seconds when suddenly, while he was making those low sounds he deeply closed his eyes and felt rising to another dimension and stopped moving and singing and remained still in peace. He was somewhere else, in a world where The fairy princess could feel his heart and mind. It was like eternity, until he opened the eyes and he could see The fairy princess on her knees closed eyes turned towards him. The power of peace was there like if they were together alone in their love dream garden both him and her resting from the world without time, space and limits. The others around didn't matter then.

The Enchanter standing felt ashamed and fell on his knees in front of her three steps from her blowing sounds for her again on his knees proving his heart love for her. Then she stood up and made a few walks closer to him and fell again on her knees two steps from him when loud high melodies of joy from the glory of his loving heart resonating in the whole room were coming out of his bamboo flute sending to The fairy princess's heart, all his mind's love, when she stood up again to grab her magical wooden flute putting herself on her knees again blowing soft melodies from her child heart.

The Enchanter felt like he had arrived to the End of his purpose and The Beginning of his True Life. Low sounds of releasement were resonating from his throat and his whole heart. Every one making sound the music tools had stopped and empty peaceful space appeared. Some of them impressed by the beauty of the revealed love of their union flames were exclaiming "Waw" Like if they had never seen or heard before anything so real. The room had reached a new place in the space...His love kingdom was expressed and her braveness had shown.

But, fast, Her prince took the Enchanter's writing string tool and told the Enchanter "Your string plastic tool is out of tune" The Enchanter didn't care about his words but stayed polite and said "Anyways, none of the music tools here are in perfect tune with the others, that is the power of the sincere heart making the melodies" And somebody handed to The fairy princess one other empty wooden little box that was in that living place which was not hers and she began to make soft heart melodies with her gentle fingers, when the Enchanter started writing words with his lips in the air in the most famous language of all the kingdoms of all times, and those words were for The fairy princess, but she didn't know. Her prince went to grab the little paper box the Enchanter had bought for her and started making also some sounds at the same time as she was. The Enchanter was annoyed by Her prince but didn't pay attention to him and kept sending words in melodies to The fairy princess, when a gentle man grabbed The fairy princess' shoulder from her back. She turned her head to that man who made a hug to her to express he was leaving the gathering. Her fingers were not making any more gentle melodies because her attention was held by that man. The Enchanter found his heart feelings cut from breath and could not express to her his heart and mind anymore. Her prince was still making The fairy princess little paper box sound. The Enchanter was no longer singing. The fairy princess after stood up and let the Enchanter on his knees alone on the floor and went to sit on the couch and made a hens of look at him. He felt like standing to go sit be sides her but Her prince went faster to sit on the floor right in front of her legs in between the Enchanter and her. The same gentleman who had started the game in circle started to make his rhythm and poems. The Enchanter found himself showing his back to that gentle man. He didn't know what to do so he made a small loop siting on the floor and turned to that gentle man and The fairy princess's prince told him "Let's go!" Most of the guests had already left and not more than eleven were still there...The fairy princess, Her prince, the Enchanter and all others still there, stood up and went on to the hall to get ready to leave the place.

While the Enchanter was putting his coat on, fast The fairy princess went in front of him to dress with her coat and they started speaking a little as their mind were always attracted to each other, so he was trying to explain to her something about music tools, as he was always, when she said "Oh so you will tell me when your dancing beauty strings shows with that other princess will happen?" They had often different thoughts crossing their mind not synchronized. He wasn't sure if she was feeling jalousie, but he replied "I am talking about something else now" But she didn't want to hear...They were both close to each other in the corner where their coats were. When the Enchanter was ready, he turned to the door but the other guests still there were in the middle and The fairy princess went besides him, and the rhythm and poems speech gentle man started asking him "And can you tell us Enchanter, why you are in our kingdom?" He felt threatened because he knew that the invisible forces had brought him there to free The fairy princess from Her prince delivering her the melodies hidden in her kingdom heart and bring her everywhere Enchant the world so everyone in all kingdoms would hear and see her beauty peace kingdom melodies and her wrists dance moves, so he just answered quickly showing to them his flute "I am here because of this little plastic flute, if this little plastic flute did not exist, I wouldn't be here" And then again he got asked "But, why you come in our kingdom if it's so cold in winter?" And he answered "Cold is my best friend and blowing sad melodies on the cold air with my trumpet is my favorite satisfaction" And again he got asked "Where in fact are you from?" And another gentle man who had heard about him replied for him "I have heard that you always answer to people #from nowhere#" And the Enchanter answered "This time, I rather say let me be a mystery" And they did not know more what to ask but some words were said while all of them were slightly moving. The fairy princess was besides the Enchanter and finally the Enchanter saw a space for him to cross the door and hoped The fairy princess would follow him even though he knew Her prince would never let her and she would never exclaim that she wanted to leave with him. One gentleman besides the Enchanter said "The chicken crossed the road" So the Enchanter copied those words singing them and dancing the swing to get out of the situation like repeating and dancing on this words #and the chicken crossed the road, and the chicken crossed the road and the chicken crossed the road# When he found himself out of the hall, all the others were still inside. He did a small loop to be towards the door again and he could only see from that angle The fairy princess with unsatisfaction in her eyes and some words in rhythm and swinging sounds came out of his voice looking in her eyes like this repeating with a little dance moves #Hey bbaby baby baby swing with me, and hey bbaby baby baby swing with me, and bbaby baby swing with me# Then everyone started to get out and the Enchanter walked down the stairs to pack his wheel carrier at the main down hall. When he was putting his music tools on his tool carrier, he heard a gentle man saying a little loud "Enchanter somebody is calling you from upstairs" He gave that gentle man his attention and just said "What?" turning himself towards the stairs and there he saw The fairy princess walking fast down the stairs carrying his gloves saying "My Enchanter you forgot your gloves" His heart started beating deeply with excitement and was fulfilled with so much joy. He thought she was going to ask him to bring her with him but when she arrived down in front of him, she did not even look at him and just laid his gloves on his wheel carrier and went walking fast up the stairs to get her music tools.

When he had finished to prepare his wheel carrier, he went outside the main hall and there The fairy princess appeared on his left side and Her prince was walking beside him on his right side together going direction to the main gate out on the street where was Her prince's wheel machine.

When they got out The fairy princess was on the Enchanter's left side and Her prince's wheel machine was on the right side as Her prince. The Enchanter of the flute felt again that, The fairy princess should leave with him because the higher power put her on his left side and thought she was going to say #I want to leave with my Enchanter# but she did not and Her prince said out loud with an aggressive voice "My wheel machine is on my right side so you have to come here on my right side!"

The fairy princess did exactly what Her prince told her to. She then told Her prince "Shake his hand and we go" So Her prince shook his hand and the Enchanter felt empty after and Her prince said "Next time we may have more music tools and more music people" The Enchanter jumped in to his wheel tool and rode to his abandoned building palace.

The Legend says that after the Enchanter saw The fairy princess dance with her prince that night with a few vulgar moves, he never ever wrote poems or music words for her and stopped admiring her...She could have given him her heart and made him become a prince of writing words and writing music but she chose another path...

CHAPTER 31
THE ENCHANTER STARTS MAKING UNDERSTAND TO THE FAIRY PRINCESS HE IS HER REAL PRINCE

The day after the Enchanter sent a letter to The fairy princess saying to her "I am so happy to see you so pleased together with your prince dancing for him with so much passion, I wish you the best in your life with him" He was pretending that emotion because they agreed that they just will be friends, but in fact inside he felt destroyed to have seen her dance for Her prince. And The fairy princess replied "Well you did not see, but I was sad and jealous at the gathering because there was the previous princess that my prince was with and still loves, so I was feeling broke and sad" The Enchanter replied "You deserve to have a prince who loves you and only you with all his heart and all his mind with no other exception princess being in the middle!"

But The fairy princess did not want to hear his words and she kept arguing and turning her mind thoughts to Her prince, so he asked her in one of his letters "Why did you fall on your knees while dancing with your prince? Was it because your prince abandoned you to go see his previous princess Gintare?" She replied "We got tired of dancing and wanted both to play music and I felt good in that position on the floor" He knew she was on her knees because something happened inside of her when he sang for her but he was trying to test her...And she also wrote to him "I know the truth my prince wants to have both for himself both Gintare and myself. I cannot follow him in that way" And the Enchanter wrote her "I am angry at your prince, he makes you suffer and doesn't really love you!"

And when the he was writing her another fast letter saying #Leave your prince and leave with me who loves you totally, I will always take care of you and I will make you dance with my music pieces and my string serenades and everyone in this world will know how beautiful your dancing hand moves wrists are# The fairy princess after sent him another fast letter saying "Mindaugas has chosen me and I just need to accept that he loved Gintare before me and it's none of your busyness to get involved with my prince and I"

The Enchanter didn't send that fast letter of heart commitment and erased it forever#

Unhappy he started complaining in more letters "You always tell me your worries and then when I am trying to help you, you reject me! I didn't want to come to your gathering, I forced myself to come just to be polite" And she wrote him a letter with this words "Well if you are polite you punish yourself, and if you keep writing me that much, I will change my fast box address secret numbers so you won't be able to write me anymore" While the Enchanter was taking off his socks with one hand to make breath his feet, he was reading at the same time the words on his plastic box of her last fast letter, the little tronic string tool bracelet gift he received form her the night before broke by the hurting power of her words. The fairy princess sent him one other letter saying "Peace on you Enchanter of the flute because you really need it," And the he replied "All right, I won't go anymore at your not peaceful gatherings and hit my magical drum so you can dance with your prince! I will keep my fingers only to make serenades for Evelina's dances, don't send to my plastic box anymore, as you ordered me to not write you that much" And they stopped sending fast plastic box letters to each other. After that revolted and hurting exchange, The fairy princess went for Christmas time in a romantic trip with Her prince to the Prague, and the Enchanter stayed on her street enchanting.

Before going to see his brother in the month of november, the Enchanter had sent The fairy princess a box with his dancing tango clothes with which he wanted to make her plastic string serenades romance, the pants were dark blue like the spanish sky at night and the shirt was also dark blue with white small roses. In the box there was also a little xylophone which he was going to use to make melodies in The waltz of Vilnus. He didn't bring it in his trip, he had too many things to carry. So she informed him by a letter "I have finally received your box from Vilnus, I have come to see you where you usually are blowing your flute in front of my living place but you weren't this time" And he answered her letter "Of course I wasn't there, I only

287

start enchanting at four o'clock when the sun is away and it's dark" It was winter, so the sun was away early. For many hours they were writing slow letters to each other...

CHAPTER 32
THE ENCHANTER TRIES TO MAKE THE FAIRY PRINCESS DANCE THE TANGO OF PRAGUE IN HIS ABANDONNED PALACE

In the many letters they exchanged, the Enchanter warned her that he was going to finish writing the book of a Fairy tales for kids about their friendship so every people in the world would know what really happened between them and listen to all the music piece he wrote for her, so he wrote her the ending he thought would be the best, and it was...

#The Enchanter and The fairy princess became very good friends and in the middle of the winter he offered her to dance for his plastic string tool in his abandoned building palace living place where was a very nice echo for his serenade melodies and very nice lights for her wrists moves. Her body contour moves lit by the street light, were moving on the circle light as shadows making his finger play the melodies of his passion heart, and then on the next floor where were more circle windows and also after on the biggest room of his building where was the biggest echo until arriving at the top in the roof of his palace where he laced with creamy bracelets two wine glasses on The fairy princess' wrists with the two little pearls laced also on each wrists with two other cream bracelets, his music box commenced to play his music piece The Tango of Prague when dancing with no physical touch the moves of two passion hearts, until the wine glasses breaking on the end of the second part of the music piece leaving her wrists free for the two circle pearls to be standing, and his breaking too, to be leading her the love dance, on the third last part the Enchanter asking her if he may lead the dance would take her hands showing her the real moves of the beauty of his plastic strings melodies that were sliding their feet moves in to the snow like if the earth would not exist anymore and the black crow would arrive to lay in to the beauty of his plastic strings proclaiming the victory of love for the unite hearts in the kingdom of freedom until the sounds of the blue harp coming from the invisible glass would melt the moment in to their arms, when The Eternal Waltz would be moving them in three steps reminding the first poem he had written for her in the most famous language in the history of the whole world in the capital of her kingdom, she would realize then that The prince of her life dream was the music tramp enchanting every day in the cold winter in front of her living place#

david de la vega

But The fairy princess answered his letter asking # But what will the kids think if the princess left with a street music tramp and ran away from Her prince with whom she already had a kingdom? Do you think it is good education?

And the Enchanter then wrote her this words #The kids will laugh, they understand things better than adults, they would know The fairy princess has to leave with the prince who loved her most...

In the reality, The fairy princess went in his under road at eleven o'clock in evening bring him the box. She was dressed in gold like a real princess, and she put his box on the floor and told him "I don't want any more boxes, it's the last time I go to the post to pick your boxes" And he handed to her his Christmas gift, it was an umbrella, a beauty for her hair and a post card on which was written the words "For your deepest dream accomplishing in your dream life" On the post card was a gentleman and a lady dancing in elegant manners. The fairy princess asked him "Are you going to make a wooden room in your building?" He answered "No, it would cost too much coins and too much effort, it is already freezing up there" The fairy princess loved the material wood and disliked the plastic. She said "I also want to talk about something with you" He replied "As you wish" She started telling him "You know you said you don't want to lie to the children that will read your story and the end seems to involve my free choice and for that we are two to choose" So he retorted "Remember you told me I could do what I want and that I should listen to my heart?" And she answered "Yes but remember you told me that you did not want to lie to children?" But he answered "Yes Fairy princess do how you feel good to do"

The fairy princess started to explain him "You remember the evening of the gathering, when I left in my prince's wheel machine I felt uncomfortable in the way home on his left side and when I arrived at our living place I found the white stone that I put in between two other stones removed and I don't understand this sign" So the Enchanter tried to explain her in an indirect way that, that sign meant she had to make her freedom become without listening and following always the authority of her prince, who was in the middle all the time. "Well fairy princess you know the power of the invisible forces make threw out our whole lives some unexplainable phenomenons threw out our lives to guide us for what we have to do to follow our path and accomplish what we need to accomplish here in this earth and if we don't accomplish our path, signs are always coming back so we find our path, because the invisible forces only can help us as a never ending fountain" But The fairy princess didn't want to understand and kept talking about Her prince and the princess Gintare, who he still loved. She was

making moves like dancing with her feet, so
he asked her "Why are you moving your feet
like that you want to dance?" She answered
"No, I am cold" So he told her "Fairy princess
you have to prepare yourself for the cold with
worm socks when you go out in winter" And
she informed him "Yes but it doesn't suit my
outfit" He found her cute to come without
worm socks to speak with him in the coldest
evening of winter and just pronounced "Hum"

The Enchanter of the flute had lived many
experiences in his life and knew the meaning
of life and also what he needed to accomplish
in his life and knew every single word he
needed to say to the people who he met and
also the mission he had to accomplish in this

earth and had understood then that The fairy princess was not ready to understand all he was doing for her and she didn't want to see that he was the prince of her life so he said after some more talking "Fairy princess you have to go it's too cold for you!" And The fairy princess didn't say a word and left...she was unsure of herself even if she pretended to know what she wanted in life...

When she was gone, he had to go to the restroom but because he had to talk so long with her, his bladder was full and he had to empty it on a paper cup and there was so much that he spilled a lot in his pants...In the way to his building he felt the freeze of minus degrees from wet pants, he stopped in a hotel where the receptionist would let him wet his shirt with water to not sweat when going up to the twelfth floor to his room every night. They also let him write letters and send them from there to The fairy princess.

The Enchanter was left unsatisfied and felt he should have asked her to come dance to his abandoned palace building but he was so down because she would always talk about Her prince that it didn't come to his mind so he decided he would write her a clear letter asking her to dance for his plastic strings serenades in his abandoned palace living...

CHAPTER 33
THE ENCHANTER SENDS THE CHILD WISH TO THE BUILDING AND TO THE FAIRY PRINCESS

So when he sat in his hotel desk. Again it
crossed his mind that he should have asked
The fairy princess to come with him dance
in his abandoned building, so he wrote her
one more letter saying "Fairy princess I was
so impressed, you stayed with me and talked
with me for so long in the coldest evening of
the year of your kingdom, no other princess
has talked to me that long in that much cold
air, so I offer to you to dance for my plastic
strings finger pieces in my palace building.
Come tomorrow after eleven o'clock in the
dark, in front of the painting of The angel
sending the dream of the kids to the freedom'
be careful don't send your pride arrows to
their minds you would hurt the kid's hearts
dream...remember take the example of the

painting where the Enchanter of kids with long hair had waited all his eternity for his dream and he got sent by The fairy princess her pride arrows and she hurt his heart and his mind. Very important, bring a bottle with worm water and put on worm socks to dance in the cold"

At eleven before midnight, he was there in front of the painting waiting for one hour on a very cold night of winter...but The fairy princess didn't come.

So around midnight the Enchanter's wheel tool was without locker as every night on the building's gate. He went up to his room and made his onion soap with his gas fire like every night before sleep. He had the idea to bring a fire steel box to light a fire in. He had to prepare his room closing all the holes doors of his room so he started to bring doors from the first floor to the twelfth floor. In total he brought up around three very heavy wooden doors and one extremely heavy steel door that he placed in the hole of the ceiling of his room and left space in that hole to put the tube of worm exit air for the fire iron box. He placed also the wooden doors in the big door holes, so the worm air wouldn't scape his room and thought he needed plastic bags to join the doors to the walls so not even a slight worm air would run away his room, and fell sleep on a candle light.

In the morning, he went to take his wheel carrier and wheel tool to prepare his hands for the cold, his wheel carrier was there but his wheel tool wasn't. His wheel carrier was removed of a few walks as it fell from the wheel tool when the thieve rode the wheel tool away. He grabbed his cold steel wheel carrier with his gloved hands, put his music tools on it, and walked to where he would enchant. He went to check his letter box and read the The fairy princess' letter saying "Thank you very much my Enchanter but sorry I won't be at your meeting time, I am going instead to a worm dancing room tonight..."

So the Enchanter wrote her back a letter saying "I will be clearer, I offer you to dance for my finger plastic serenade string's moves in my palace building and if I like your soft gentle wrists beauty moves, I will bring you everywhere in the whole world dancing for every one and every people of this earth will know how beautiful hand finger moves you make and everyone will know you are The fairy princess"

The Enchanter had no more wheel tool so he went to the capital take his other wheel tool. When he had read her reply fast letter saying "Dear Enchanter, your dream sounds very good, I will be thinking about it, if that is alright for you?" his answer was, "All right my fairy princess I will be waiting"

How could a goddess send an arrow to the child if she was full of love, would it be the poison of the Scorpio in her mind and heart, or might be. . .the Enchanter's dream got hurt and his child dream got broke when he was already a strong man fighting for her, his inside child had accepted the rejection but, why to give to a painting on a wall the last word while the goddess of writing has the power to make a so magical destiny...

CHAPTER 34

THE ENCHANTER IS STOPPED FROM RECORDING HIS MASTER PIECE THE TANGO OF PRAGUE

The Enchanter was trying to make Ignas capture #The tango of Prague# because he needed to dance on the roof of his abandoned palace with The fairy princess to the master piece but Ignas was not answering. He asked Ignas one more time so he could capture his master piece #The tango of Prague# but the Enchanter had told him that he wrote all his poems and all his music pieces for The fairy princes. And Ignas cancelled the last meeting and never captured anymore his music pieces. At first he didn't understand why Ignas refused but he thought that maybe the prince Ignas knew Mindaugas The fairy princess' prince, he remembered once he saw them together so they were probably friends.

Knowing that the Enchanter had written all his music pieces for The fairy princess could be inappropriate for Ignas if he knew personally Mindaugas her prince.

The Enchanter of the flute wanted to build shoes for him and also for the fairy princess so he went to buy material and fur, but one princess did not give him back the tool that he lent to her because she liked metal tools, so he could not build the shoes for himself for the winter to protect his feet when playing his flute in the cold streets. He also needed a fire box for his room, so he went to the big house building store to look for a fire steel box for his room and saw one little one costing around one hundred eleven coins, but there was no tube available for the same shape of

exit worm air, so he reserved it. He was still
inside the big store looking at every tool to
think what he would need for the cold winter
and there he saw a princess walking with
beautiful hair pigtails, one on the left and
one on the right, it was his most favorite hair
art. He pronounced her name without being
aware of what was happening, she turned
herself and it was her The fairy princess, he
was amazed delighted and sublimed saying
"Oh it's you" And added "What are you doing
here?" And she replied "Yes it's me, I am
looking for tools I need, but I have to go" And
she walked away. He wanted to go see her
in the other room of the big tool store where
she went but thought #if she needs to go she
won't give me any time as always# and left

with his wheel tool to enchant, and earn coins for the fire box...

The day after he brought, all the coins he had earned, bought, the fire box went, to place it to his room but, he hadn't thought, that, the only way to get, inside the building was to go through the twenty fingers large gate hole going up through the three steps long stiff narrow wall recovered by ice making him slide with the heavy fire iron box When he arrived to the gate hole sound of drops were resonating in the entire building, the ice was melting by the magical power of the invisible forces, the temperature had fallen up to more than zero degrees and he could walk up the three steps long stiff narrow wall without, any effort and get, inside the gate hole. His fire iron box was very hard to get in and there was only the exact space between the parts of the gate so he was moving the heavy fire box looking for the right angle to get it in. He managed to bring it in by two finger wide.

He brought the heavy fire steel box until the twelfth floor and put it in the spot he thought was the best and sat making sound fingers with his plastic string tool.

As planned the day after he went to buy the tube exit metal piece for the fire iron box and also the plastic past to gather them and fulfilled the space. After blowing his flute in his underground Transition, he went to his building and when he was in the twelfth floor room, he put the paste correctly around the exit tube so it would hold and placed the big long tubes that were there in the building so the smoke could get out from the fire box properly, and then connected the strong tube exit and the long tube leading the smoke out from his room and finally lit the fire. He then had the first night fire, grabbed his plastic string tool and while making his onion soup he sang passion words on serenades for The fairy princess who was not there, after he fell asleep on a candle light.

The Enchanter had noticed while moving his fingers for the sounds of his plastic string tool that the air was running away from him, so while blowing his flute in his under music road Transition he was asking to the people passing by, if they could buy for him plastic bags cause he needed them to fulfil the space between the wooden doors and the cold walls. A nice gentle man stopped with his lady and went to buy the plastic bags and refused to take the Enchanter's coins. He wanted to buy them with his own coins and brought many, more than thirty three so the Enchanter had then way enough bags to prevent the air from running away from his heated room. When he arrived that night to his twelve floor room after having lit the fire steel box, he placed all the plastic bags in the places where air was flowing inside and could move his fingers for his plastic string tool in a wormer air.

CHAPTER 35
THE FAIRY PRINCESS TELLS THE ENCHANTER HIS DREAMS ARE NOT THAT IMPORTANT

If this story is almost exact, the day after or two days after, the Enchanter was under his music underground Transition on the left side and The fairy princess passing by from his right side told him "I can't stop for you, keep playing your flute don't stop" He kept playing until he noticed that it was smelling like dog urine so he changed his place to the other side. One hour after, The fairy princess was passing again from his right side, he was on her left side. He didn't stop blowing his flute until she was on his left side and when then she quit walking the melodies coming from his flute were silent, she had the space then to tell him "Why did you change from that side to this side?" And he answered "It doesn't smell so good there, I should clean it tomorrow" She then said "Interesting it's cold I am tired and I am going to my living place." Before she made her first step, he asked her "Fairy princess have you thought of dancing on my abandoned palace you won't regret it, I have brought now the fire iron box in there, so you can worm your cold feet, if you come" And she answered "Dear Enchanter of all the flutes of the world, why do you ask me that now?" He answered "Because you wrote in your letter that you would think about it" So she replied "Oh well I haven't thought about it and maybe I won't think about it" So he told her "Fairy princess do you have dreams?" And she retorted "Dreams don't need to be accomplished" So he said "The night I brought the heavy fire steel box, in the third floor while caring it up I had a vision of your writs moving gently with the shape of your body's contour sculpturing the shadow on a circle light coming from the circle window and your arms writs moves were more than beautiful making my fingers sound the beauty of the plastic strings of my string tool" She retorted "You should not stick on your visions" Very unhappy he told her "All right fairy princess go with your prince in your worm living place, take care of him and leave me alone in my cold" And she left...

A few days after when the Enchanter was in peace in the cold snowed street enchanting with his plastic flute, both the street and the garden, The fairy princess and Her princess appeared holding food bags holding, and Her prince said "We have good news for you, my princess and I are starting to show our dances to other dancers who want to copy us, we will teach them, we are such a delightful couple" The Enchanter was extremely unhappy but didn't say a word...And Her prince asked "How is your skills in our kingdom language going?" The Enchanter answered "Ne sprotu ko tu saki." which meant, "I don't understand what you're saying" Because he had learnt the neighbor's kingdom languages that had the same root as their kingdom languages. The Enchanter unhappy was not talkative so they left.

CHAPTER 36
THE ENCHANTER ASKES THE FAIRY PRINCESS TO NOT COME SEE HIM WHEN BEING WITH HER PRINCE

The Enchanter's dream of dancing with The fairy princess got stolen by a faster prince than him so the unhappiness fulfilled his heart and decided he would send a letter to The fairy princess saying "Fairy princess you come to me to show the joy to have chosen your prince to make you dance, so I ask you please to not approach me anymore when you are with him, our friend ship has no meaning my dreams and my visions don't mean to you and they are the most important for me and I do everything to make them real in my life cause I know I came in this world for that reason, I have respected your choice to forbade me to not send to your plastic box fast letters and I have respected your command as you can notice, and I write you this demand in your slow letter box for you to respect the choice I made so you don't come to me with your prince anymore. If you want to hear the exact real truth, I don't feel satisfaction from him holding your hand but unhappiness, so may you respect my wish and I hope for you the most happy life with him, as you noticed I lent to him my magical drum so you can share your heart melodies with him" And The fairy princess answered his letter saying...

"If it doesn't please you to see us in our street then why do you stay nearby where we live... I won't hold back my joy if it's full of good feelings just because you suffer, in order to make you happy. My prince cares for you getting cold with his good heart and you hold anger and jealousy for him. One other thing, when we spoke that cold night, of the winter, the so cold evening when I got cold, I thought we could be friends and go for a tea and just talk but now, I see that you lied to me, that you don't have feelings for me, if you would care for me only just as friends you wouldn't feel those feelings you feel now, you try to own me while no body owns me"

And he answered "I was there playing my flute before meeting you. When I arrived in your kingdom it was a new beginning in my life and had joy inside and you came in my life, I thought you were unsatisfied princess and I sent to you all the emotions I had for you on paper and in writing words, my heart screamed in front of your living place and in all places of your street how strong and big was my passion for you and you never noticed me or came alone while I was saving all my coins blowing on my ears until even hurting my tympanums and freezing my fingers on the cold to buy for you all the tools you needed to make sound your heart melodies and also all the dresses you deserved to wear, so you could stand your beauty while I was spilling my tears in silence alone for you. You prince caring for me getting cold, hah as I am a passionate tramp since more than seven years who knows all the corner of all the streets in the world as good as you know your bath, it sounds so not honest and not true from him, sorry but I don't see or feel those fake feelings he has. All right your happiness is to be with him, your choice is to give him your heart for his pride, joy and glory...When you talked to me in the other dimension time I thought for you the emotions were more important than the comfort, I apologize I was mistaken. Talk in a worm place for a tea, I don't believe you, you have never kept any promise you made to me because you are always busy holding the hands of whom, that prince who cares for me getting cold, that sounds like a joke. You never came to the capital to see me while you said many times you would, you know first time I met your prince, he told me #you have to show to woman that you can give them comfort so they will want to be with you# it is when I started not liking him because for me a princess is not a whore who just needs a bed and worm food and be payed where ever she goes because she looks good with a skirt but she is a mind and a heart that has melodies inside and needs to blow them for the glory of her beauty heart...that doesn't matter to you as I can see. You told me no one owns you, but you do everything your prince tells you to when he commands you to and makes you move like he wants you to in life like in dancing. You are trying to make me believe that you forced him to command to you to go always with him and never follow me...That makes you a liar because you said you would have brought me to a warm place for tea while you would have just listened to his commandments and refused to come to me if he told you to not to. It is not important anymore if you don't understand my words...

but today I just want to feel joy inside and stop punishing myself. You told me you would come to Vilnus to see me, and you never did. You haven't much done for me in fact, except making food for me twice because your prince brought me to your living place, and offered me the little toy string tronic tool as if I was a child and the hand key little piano while I need a real piano to offer my melodies. I was lying to myself, believing that you will bring me a hot tea when blowing my flute in the cold and you threw away all the dresses I bought for you...

Now that you have made me realize that I was punishing myself if I be polite, I tell you all my thoughts straight without politeness and you accuse me to be a liar, I never lied to you, this game may be funny for you, and you don't wonder if it is funny for me but remember all I have sent you with my coins or the people's coins thrown at me but you may not see the value. You forced me to be happy for all your choices, so now you know the unrevealed Truth...As you know I was everywhere looking for you in all corners and now that I found you, you just choose another prince instead of me but I love my life, so I survive, the worst is that you claim that I don't have feelings for you...Your statement awoke the truth so fulfil yourself with the truth..."

The fairy princess replied his letter like this "Well listen, I have never told you to buy clothes for me is that right, but I understand your tears I was once also suffering before I met, My prince but, now sorry to tell you but, I love him and I will stay with him I choose him no matter what, so you can cry, scream with your magical drum, say whatever you want, but, it, doesn't touch my heart. We were living in this place before you came so if you are not, happy with that, you can go enchant, the kids somewhere else. I truly wanted to speak with you with drink in warm place but, if you don't, believe me it's your choice" The Enchanter of the flute replied to her that, he did not, believe her anymore, because she had promised and said that, she will do things with him but, never came and in the last, letter The fairy princess wrote him "I will not, allow anymore your slow letters to arrive to my heart, I will forbade them in my heart, and my mind" And she added "You expected me to leave my prince for you just because you claimed to love me, you are so ridiculous"

So then now, the Enchanter had delivered his broken heart to The fairy princess and she knew he felt the unhappiness from seeing her with Her prince and had asked her to convince Her prince to interrupt him while he was enchanting cause he needed no help for cold and needed no friendly words from his voice while he was doing everything to steal from him The fairy princess of his life. This clash was a hard moment for him, but that was not all, the bad cigar disgusting schizophrenic arrogant man was starting to come harassing him every night late when not much people were passing by, telling him "You cannot be here go somewhere else... this is not your kingdom go back from where you come..." That horrible creature man would come smoke his cigar in front of him making smoke that he couldn't stand. The Enchanter would tell him nicely "Excuse me, please I don't stand the smell of cigar, I am allergic please could you go away from me please, I need to blow my flute melodies in peace I need air for my lungs" But that disgusting man would laugh with loud arrogant sounds of voice and stay there in front of him with his cigar for sometimes more than one hour, until one day he stood up grabbed him by his cloths and was moving him with all his wrath until the guards came to separate them...

The Enchanter had noticed that arrogant man had two personalities, he would come with a leather jacket as a crappy person and attack him mocking him and sometimes he would pass by dressed with a suit looking like a respectful gentle man with a hat on his head caring briefcase. That person was sick and had a double personality, his mind was full of insanity. The Enchanter was receiving attention, many young princesses were every half an hour bringing him a cup of hot water to warm his fingers.

Two evenings later the Enchanter of the flute was blowing his flute the dark and cold street of The fairy princess near the fruit store, when she and Her prince were coming from the fruit store. He ignored them but

Her prince approached him and said "Labas" Which meant good evening in their language. The Enchanter felt again very bad like an invisible poison was with Her prince's word "Labas" He could not blow his flute anymore, his heart felt like paralyzed but later that evening, he met a princess and they talked about living together in a new building.

CHAPTER 37
THE ENCHANTER ASKES AGAIN TO THE FAIRY PRINCESS TO BE LEFT ALONE AND FINDS OUT SHE HAS FEELINGS FOR HIM

As The fairy princess had forbidden the Enchanter's slow letter in her heart, he used the other option, a fast letter, "Fairy princess you commended me to not send you anymore fast letters anymore or you will forbade them from your heart, I demanded to you to not come around me or talk to me when you are with your prince over three walks from me. You have forbid my slow letters from arriving to your heart, and I have as you see respected your commandment, so I ask you for second time to respect my wish to not make me be involved in a conversation with your prince. He carries his scorpio poison from November to send at me, I don't have an appropriate protection for that, as my heart is totally opened, and you who is supposed to proclaim my melodies' victory are on his side. You can tell him that, I need to be alone and he will be fine as you are his trophy what else does he want from me... There is nobody in your kingdom telling me good evening and I prefer and appreciate people not giving me attention, I like to feel lost and alone. People can tell me good things but inside caring an invisible poison to fulfil my heart with that poison. I don't believe in good empty wishes but in true real actions...I believe intentions can send a healthy love or an invisible poison, So please you can come this evening pick the letter for your prince,, he may understand my wish after reading my letter, I am writing one for you too. I will be waiting for you to pick them up tonight, so you will be able to read him his letter"

The fairy princess answered to his fast letter box "Don't be waiting for me my dear Enchanter, I may come like I may not come. Do what you want but don't wait for me, I love Mindaugas and will only come with him together" So the Enchanter of the flute wrote her "You are so selfish" She didn't appreciate that reply and she retorted "Oh let's be clear, you say I am selfish because you are always waiting for me. You think I should come for you and I don't agree with you that I am The flame of your fire melodies and don not come live my life with you, choosing my happiness over yours?" He answered her "I think you are selfish because you think I am always waiting for you while my music happens by the power of my heart, and my mind, I think you are waiting for yourself to be true to yourself...oh yeah easy comfort... and I believe that you love more the living place and the comfort that you have with your prince than his mind and his heart."

Of course the Enchanter was holding up his sweet feelings and pretending he was strong because in fact he was always wishing that The fairy princess would come see him where his enchanting places...

Then The fairy princess unsure wrote him "I thought you were always waiting for me, that is what you wrote me many times, did you or I imagined?"

The Enchanter of the flute was writing the letter for her and preparing the gift, which was a pair of warm real sheep wool socks that he put in the same kind of box that The fairy princess used to offer to him the little piano key handle for the Christmas gift, it was a box of the color gold. In the box, he also put a transparent crystal pendulum, so she could ask questions to The invisible forces and have the confirmation of the truth. After he went to the old town enchant with his flute, and saw The fairy princess sent him the last fast letter so he answered her saying "That I am waiting always for you means that you can come at any moment...Oh I thought it was a letter from my new princess and not, it's the letter of the sweet Fairy princess who loves to fight in letters, with mind words and heart emotions" The fairy princess got hurt and answered his fast letter "All right, if I annoy you that much, I will stop writing you" And the Enchanter got moved in his heart and got tendered again by her reply, and wrote her "I never said that you annoy me, don't you think I would fight with word on letters if I wouldn't like it, don't you think I would blow my plastic flute if I wouldn't enjoy it?" So The fairy princess's pride came back to her heart because she felt he still loved her and she answered "Oh my dear Enchanter you are interrupting my work with your fast letters"

CHAPTER 38
THE FAIRY PRINCESS FINALLY RECEIVES THE HARP THE ENCHANTER SENT HER

Later he received a fast letter saying "Dear Enchanter I was there in your place looking for you to take the letter for my prince and you weren't there...And I want to thank you to have bought me an arfa...I receive it today, I really did not expect it" And he wrote her back "You can come now, I am back, I just went to buy candles, the harp I thought you already had it, it took a long time to arrive to you then" And she answered "I will not come, I took a bath and my hair is wet and it's freezing outside, I don't want to get sick for tomorrow I have writing exam" So the Enchanter wrote her "I can come to your door to give you the letters in hands, so you don't stay inside and just give them to you from the door" And she replied with pride "Don't

Enchanter, keep playing your flute, we will come with my prince when we will have time, I won't come alone but my prince may come himself tonight take his letter if he feels like" The Enchanter didn't reply cause he knew The fairy princess was always playing with his emotions and she sent some other words to him saying "Is it fine for you if my prince comes without me?" Then he replied "I would rather that you come than him, your prince puts some heavy lead feelings in my heart that are not beautiful, he makes me feel like poisoned" So she retorted "Dear Enchanter don't cry like a child, be a man" So he replied "Why then you ask me, if you don't care about my heart feelings?" And she answered "Dear Enchanter, I already told you, we will not come until we want to and I won't come alone but with my prince, I don't think your letters are that important." The Enchanter went to his Transition enchant with his flute until late midnight and her prince did not come, and he wrote her "No princess came tonight and no real man either." But it was very late and she did not reply, so he went to his twelve floor room.

The day after he checked his fast letters, he had received one saying "I told you we will come when we want not when you want."

As he was planning to change his spot and enchant somewhere else and instead of her street he answered "The letters don't matter if you respect my wish to not come see me with your prince everything will be all right."

CHAPTER 39
THE LAST ENCHANTER'S LETTER
FOR THE FAIRY PRINCEESS

Three weeks later the Enchanter wrote to The fairy princess, the most aggressive letter of all,

This is the last fast letter I send you and after I will erase your plastic box address and will never write you anything ever again and I will disappear from your life, remember when I asked you to come see me in Vilnus, and you said you will but you went to the gathering festival with your prince and there was an enormous wind those two days of the gathering, I know that because when there is enormous wind as you know I am a tramp and homeless who experiences all the winds in the year. You wrote me, that it was a challenge for you to be camping during that

wind, well it was not a challenge and not me who was angry as you accused me to be but the wrath of invisible forces of power who cause you were supposed to come see me and make melodies with me but you did not. The invisibles forces are alive and react when you are not doing what you are supposed to, that power cannot always force people but have power over the wind, the rain the clouds the temperature and many other phenomenon, remember when you went to Nida and I was asking you to let me come with you and coldly you refused, the storm that appear when you were on the beach at night... It wasn't either my personal anger as you often said it was but the invisible power's wrath because you did not what you were supposed to. How can a man have anger if he is sad. . .But here comes my peace and love captured in a last, fast, letter #

After that letter was sent, he sent her a music piece called Autumn call, captured with the three poems in the most famous language for her and he also sent another one music piece called 'the Shaman girl' for her to play her magical wooden flute on it, they were on the same pitch on C minor. He wrote words on the letter like this. . ."If you answer me thank you, I will send you one more song, but, The fairy princess did not reply"

The day after while he was talking to a pretty princess, The fairy princess's prince passed by and laid one cracking food beside his coin basket, so in the same afternoon the Enchanter went to his office to talk to him, and he asked him "Would it be possible that you don't come to me anymore for any reason? I don't feel good about your princess. She and I are not friends anymore. And the pendulum has told me that she was the fairy princess of my life" Her prince answered "Maybe so, but she is with me hah" He mocked him about his trust in the pendulum and added "So you pretend we are not allowed to walk by in our street?" The Enchanter answered "You can go anywhere you want, but when you see me, just take her by her hand and bring her to your living place as she is with you but don't come to me, I don't feel good when you control what her heart will wants" Her prince would not understand how much the Enchanter was suffering and told him "If you

suffer, it's your choice, it's your problem" So
the Enchanter asked "So you think she is the
Princess of your life?" And Her prince started
talking about his precious Gintare "Well I love
Gintare, but I think we can be with someone
long time with a certain connection, yes now
yes, she is a good princess" So the Enchanter
of the flute saw that her prince clearly was
totally confused talking about his previous
princess Gintare while the main topic was
The fairy princess but he was sure that it was
useless to talk with him because he gave more
value to his personal glory than the emotions
of others. Her prince added "You want to put
a word on my connection with her but with us
is beyond everything" The Enchanter wanted
to leave and said "Hey I may come take back

my magical drum soon I want to hit it again,,
I will go now" Her prince said "I would like to
buy it," And the Enchanter replied "You can
find many others, there are a lot of them out
there, there is even a builder in your town"
But her prince said "Maybe but from you
it will be cheaper, so I can save coins" He
understood then why Her prince tolerated him
offering so many gifts to his princess, then it
was cheaper, as he would spend all his coins
buying gifts for her.

CHAPTER 40
THE ENCHANTER AND THE FAIRY PRINCESS START IGNORING EACH OTHER

The Enchanter of the flute had decided that he would be the less possible in The fairy princess's street and was then instead every afternoon from four o'clock in the cold dark until sometimes nine or later in another place in the old town...On a Sunday he saw The fairy princess walking there and he thought that she passed so he would see her ignoring him but then he saw Her prince passing by the same day and later around ten in the evening they passed together holding hands, they had understood his wish and finally were ignoring him as he had asked them. But he was seeing them passing by turning every time in the street corner always in front of where he was enchanting and found out that dancing classes were happening in that street, so he understood that they were dancing there a few times a week. So every time The fairy princess and Her prince would pass by his new place, the Enchanter would see them and feel oppressed inside.

In the day of saint valentine there was a strong sun for a winter, and a young princess called Oguste came to him. After he had told her the way he was living, she told him she wanted to travel with him, but she was only fourteen, it was too young for her to live like him. She told him she wanted to have a pig, so he was going to buy a pig to have company when enchanting with his flute. When they passed by his building Oguste wanted to go up to the top cause she was dreaming about it as she already noticed the building since some time but he told her they could go another time, but she insisted so he accepted to bring her up. He made his onion soup in front of her, and then she wanted to visit the roof. When they were up the flat roof, she had to go sot= the Enchanter brought her to where she took the big wheel machine for her to go home.

Two weeks later Oguste came to see him with a friend of her who told the Enchanter "If you love Oguste, buy for her illegal drinks, we want to get drunk, we are not allowed to buy for our self's we are way too young" The Enchanter refused and was disappointed that they just wanted to use him to get illegal drinks. Then he fell sick in the middle of the winter, he did not put his pullover during the night and slept in the cold. He was very week but still he was enchanting every day with his flute, when a not nice man came to attack him while he was preparing the basket to receive coins and eating at the same time. He had no energy and was very week but he retaliated with power. That other arrogant, crappy cigar man was there at that moment and saw the Enchanter being attacked. One other person came to separate them and that violent bad person left and the guards arrived but there was one guard who was mean and did not accept the Enchanter reporting the attack to the kingdom cancel.

The evening after at almost midnight that disgusting man appeared and with his feet kicked the Enchanter's coin basket. All his coins were sent away and the Kuna coin went in to the sewers. The Enchanter just looked at him in the eyes, and the crappy man also hit his flute with his hand from left to right, His flute was sent away. Standing fast the Enchanter pushed strongly that crappy man away, and took his wheel carrier to defend himself because he was so week and sick. People were passing by and he was screaming "Please call the guards! Please call the guards! Help me!" But nobody would help him, until two nice young princesses felt him and went out the Transition and called the guards who came, but again, came that mean guard. The Enchanter asked him "I would like to declare this attack to the council of the kingdom" But that mean guard said again "Sorry I will not help you" and left.

CHAPTER 41
THE ENCHANTER OF THE FLUTE THINKS THE FAIRY PRINCESS IS JEALOUSE

One evening there, in his new place the Enchanter of the flute was talking with the nice princess with who he was going to live who borrowed his steel string music tool. She came to give it back to him and tell him they weren't going to live together. He noticed The fairy princess was passing by with Her prince. When they had passed his place and were back towards him. He noticed carefully The fairy princess wouldn't let Her prince take her hand even though he was insisting trying to grab her hand but she wouldn't let him hold her by her hand. She was putting her hands in her coat, so the Enchanter felt that The fairy princess was unsatisfied because she saw him with another princess and she was used to being his whole attention as if Her prince was not enough for her to be totally happy...The Enchanter thought, The fairy princess was jealous because she saw him with another princess. He could not be sure but it was his feeling, her refusing to hold Her prince's hand was strange...

In the same evening the Enchanter had finished to enchant and was going back to his abandoned palace and was besides the river rolling his wheel tool feeling sadness in his way back when he saw The fairy princess walking but he did not stop and kept riding. A few walks after the invisible forces made him stop, and he remained still with closed eyes feeling. Then he turned his head back but she was no longer there, she had crossed the bridge and was in the island park where he had written all the poems for her. He felt he had to go there too. When arrived in the island, he left his wheel tool with the wheel carrier at the kinder park and went to the bridge to blow his flute. The fairy princess passed by him ignoring him when he was blowing a melody to the water. He then saw her when she had crossed the bridge walking her way. He felt she was scared of him. He felt far away from her path.

CHAPTER 42
THE FAIRY PRINCESS' PRINCE
FINALLY RESPECT THE ENCHANTER'
WILL TO BE ALONE

For two months, the Enchanter of the flute and The fairy princess were ignoring each other. With Her prince, they were passing by in front of the Enchanter going to their dance classes. They had understood and respected his wish to not be approached by them but it was hard for him to ignore her. He would feel pressure in his heart seeing her pass by with Her prince and having to ignore her...

When it was starting to be wormer as the winter was almost over, one evening coming from the old town going probably to her living place, The fairy princess passed by him. He forced himself to not stop blowing his flute when he saw her, but he felt almost his loving heart burst...

The spring had started and he had to go back to see his brother and had decided that he would take back the magical drum he had lent to The fairy princess's prince. He wanted to enchant hitting melodies with it. He had realized he had been too nice to them. That day The fairy princess passed by in front of him while he was there by her living place She was not going to her living place like she would have been supposed to. The Enchanter felt she was trying to get back his attention because she was tired of being ignored by him but he was determined to keep ignoring her. So when she was passing by slowly right close to him, he made the effort to not look at her even though he had seen her coming.

She made a little sign to him with her hand but he stayed strong and they did not speak.

Later in the same day he went to see. Her prince and asked back his magical drum. Her prince told him that he will come bring it to him after work. The Enchanter of the flute was there waiting but for him, but he did not come. So two days after, he went back to his office and told him that he really wanted to have back his magical drum and Her prince said "Sorry I forgot to come the other day, you can come this evening to our living place at eight o'clock, I will give it to you" And he was there at eight o'clock but Her prince was not. So he understood that he was playing with him. He entered in side their building and waited by the stairs until eleven o'clock blowing his bamboo traversal flute in the dark when he heard her voice, suddenly The fairy princess opened the door, Her prince and her were getting inside, talking and laughing as if they were a drunk. The Enchanter of the flute was by stairs with his wheel tool and his wheel carrier. When she saw him she got scared because he was in the dark and his bamboo melodies were resonating in on the walls of the stairs. Her prince told her "Go upstairs" And also told the Enchanter the same but the Enchanter took some time to organize his wheel carrier making space for the magical drum. Seeing The fairy princess, made him dizzy but he went up anyways. Her prince handed him his magical drum and he handed to Her prince the bag with the gifts for The fairy princess saying "This is for your her" It was the two letters with the warm sheep wool sucks he had bought for her, the crystal pendulum and the little tiny piano handle key with a little phrase written on a paper saying #I prefer to open my heart, it is the only key of my destiny# The fairy princess was in the living room but as soon as she heard her name she came at the door and took her gifts. As soon as the Enchanter crossed her eyes and saw that she had the gifts bag in her hands, he left right away going down the stairs.

The Enchanter of the flute went to hide his plastic string tool in his building and his gas cooking spray, and the bag with the baby blue dress for The fairy princess. Only then he started his trip to his brother.

CHAPTER 43
THE ENCHANTER OF THE FLUTE
FINS HIS BLACK CROW

The day after he started the big trip to his brother. He stopped in a big town in the late night. It was windy and cold, he had just a light cover and was walking in the old town. He saw a church opened. He got inside, closed the door and slept inside. The day after, in the morning he bought two magical flutes one plastic which he called #my black crow# it was the flute of The tango of Prague and the other he called #the owl# it was the flute of The waltz of Vilnus. When he arrived to his youth town, he went to see his friend with psychic abilities and he was told that he needed to speak to The fairy princess...They asked to the pendulum to get confirmation of the invisible forces truth, and the forces in the pendulum indicated yes, the same as his psychic friend would say, she was testing him to check if he really held in to her…When he had his psychic friend advices and the pendulum's confirmation he said good bay to his brother and his donkeys and then he left. This time he had no wheel tool, just his flutes a bag and a soft cover. He was crossing the kingdoms with strong wheel power machines going fast until he arrived to a place called Innsbruck where he was getting lot of coins when blowing his black crow and his 7 coins plastic flute to enchant the kids passing by but that kingdom's guards came to tell him "You have to give us fifty coins or we take all your flutes, you have not declared your enchantment to our cancel as you should have" Of course he gave them fifty coins because all his flutes were the most important he owned, he didn't want to lose them.

The day after he found an abandoned wheel tool so he was waiting more than three hours in order to be sure it wasn't anybody's who had gone to the restroom and left it there for some time. When he had waited enough, he approached the wheel tool and noticed the wheel tool had no chain, it was steel heavy wheel tool so he understood somebody had abandoned it. In that kingdom people had many coins in their banks and could afford new ones. There, many rusting wheel tools were abandoned but he took that one because he was sure it was the invisible forces had chosen it for him. He went to put a chain to a wheel tool garage and then continued his trip.

He was crossing lands. He found himself following a river with besides rocky hills for thousands walks long. He passed by many villages enchanting and was feeling he was finally going to conquer his fairy princess with the power of his new black crow victory flute's melodies.

He arrived to a called Landshut and found two other flutes which he called #the little happy bird and the bird on the tree# And bought five golden little bird flutes for The fairy princess and one green other to offer her at first and he also bought three brown flutes all of the same family color because he wanted to create a flute and magical drum school in the old town of The fairy princess kingdom. He also passed by the kingdom where he was threaten last time Krakovia and managed to make some coins before the guards came to tell him he needed to go pay the taxes to their kingdom before being able to enchant the people there. After riding his wheel tool for days, he arrived to the kingdom called Varsovia and there were too many people singing while at the same time playing string tools so he had no space free in the air to blow his melodies, so he made a few coins where nobody was and left to join The fairy princess kingdom.

CHAPTER 44
THE FAIRY PRINCESS SHOWS HER UNSTIFACTION BECAUSE OF THE ENCHANTER IGNORING HER

When he arrived to destination, he felt so released and so good with enjoyment inside and took one of his new flutes called the bird of the tree and blowing melodies he felt The fairy princess was not far. From his left came a strange feeling and he looked there and he saw her wearing a dark soft green pants the same color as his tshirt but she went straight away to a tea saloon, and he kept enchanting with his bird flute with inside joy but he didn't see when she went out of the tea salon He kept blowing his melodies. When the sun was almost gone, he felt some strange feeling from his right side and turned his head to the right and The fairy princess was there walking slowly with one other princess friend of hers but he kept blowing, and when she arrived three walks from him, he felt her again, he turned his head again but, didn't stop blowing on his flute, and when finally she was in front of him, he felt her presence and turned his eyes up and their eyes crossed. She was making a hand sign to him as she always did, but he kept blowing oppressing his heart in order to show he was strong. A few seconds after he felt dizzy because it was too strong emotion and he rested his back on the street lamp like out of mind dropping his chin on his chest down sinking on his inside waves losing control of his mind...After a few seconds passed he felt a strange feeling coming from his left and an adrenaline made his head turn to the left, The fairy princess was alone turned like staring at him without her friend besides. She was moving a gate with her hands making the gate's metal bars knock the gate metal bars as if she was oppressed demanding his attention. As soon as she noticed him looking at her, she turned back to the other side and kept walking until disappearing in the end of the street's corner. The Enchanter then realized that The fairy princess was all tired of ignoring one another and she was really willing to speak with him again...

The day after, it was a very sunny and the Enchanter changed his place to the other side of the street to be hiding himself from the sun and be on the shadow. He was enchanting with his black crow, and noticed The fairy princess walking slowly. She was far from him like almost walking touching the wall of the other side of the street. He felt like she was sad or upset because he would ignore her without rest. She went directly to her living place without making and sign to him. Later he changed his side and was positioned as usual but still blowing on his black crow flute with peace, when suddenly, he felt a feeling of tenderness and couldn't blow anymore on his black crow, The fairy princess had passed by, she was wearing her black dress with cuts on each side from her feat to her hips she wore the evening of the gathering when he saw her dancing for Her prince. She was then walking toward the fruit store until getting inside. As it was a big releasement for him to blow his black crow flute, he had no longer in mind that The fairy princess had gotten inside the shop and was not aware anymore that she was going to pass by him again on her way back to her living place, and he was blowing his black crow with satisfaction and nostalgia, when he felt this soft feeling and turned fast his head to the left, The fairy princess was walking quick, she was waving her hand to him, he also not in purpose lifted his hand discreetly and she understood that was a sign for her to go to him because that was the way she understood hand signs. She approached very close like determined, a little up tied and first asked "Do you want to speak with me?" When he answered something like "Why not" He was very calm and slow and it was taking him some time to pronounce his thoughts because his mind and his heart were tired of her undecided behavior and his trip had made him feel released. Fast he remembered what he planned to ask her and he asked her "Do you still like your wooden flute I bought you?" And fast she answered "Yes I still like it, at first I didn't like them all but now I like all the flutes you bought for me and know how to blow on them all, but I don't know how to make melodies" He was surprised with her tone but did not realize what she meant because he was slow in his mind after his long wheel tool rolling trip, and said "Oh nice if you still like them I have many other new ones, I know you don't like plastic but where I bought this wooden flute, I saw this bag and thought about your wooden magical flute and bought it for you because I care for your flute and it would be nice if you would have a protection bag" Almost interrupting him she said "I don't need it, I plan to sew one myself, keep it for your flutes you need it" Then he showed her the wooden flute that he had bought for her and blew a little on it to show her how nice the flute sounded and asked "You like it?" She liked it so she answered "Waw, it sounds so nice!" With a spice of excitement...and he said "Then you can try it" But she couldn't make melodies with it and as he had bought it for her he said "Well, if you like it, you can have it" But she answered "Keep it for yourself" He did not insist and then he took a bird green nature little flute and let her try it "You can try this one too" And she tried that one too, but she couldn't blow melodies, she wasn't use to that bird flute either. Then he took it back and blew his melody out of the bird flute and she was amazed by how pretty his melodies sounded. He tried to give her that little flute "Keep it, if you try alone, melodies will come out of this bird green flute, trust on the magi, you just have to try" And again The fairy princess refused to have that bird flute, and he did not insist. After he asked him "Do you have something else to ask me?" He thought strongly and remembered he had been asked by his friend very rich prince of the capital to go up to his new building to talk to his twenty advisors responsible for the order of the manufacture of his goods and told her "You know, I have been asked to speak about the power of the invisible forces in a friend prince's new building because he thinks my way of living is interesting and I thought you could come with me there and touch your plastic harp strings with your mind love while I enchant with my flute and you can blow on your traversal silver flute when I make romance with my plastic string tool beauty sounds and you also can blow on your magical wooden flute when I hit the glory of the melodies of my magical drums, you also can play with them if you want" And The fairy princess answered "I can only blow on the flutes, I have told you but I can't make melodies" So he said "But it's very easy you just need to blow with your heart and move your fingers and the magi will happen" But she replied "I am not ready to make melodies in front of people, I like to make sounds for myself and I don't make melodies" And he insisted saying "But there will not be more than twenty persons" And she said then "I will think about it" And she left. He was hearing a sort of tango music piece in his mind. Later up in his abandoned palace he found that piece on his plastic string tool, it was #The tango of Diane#

The last talk with The fairy princess made him sad because he knew she said she did not make melodies to hurt his loving heart and felt it was useless to make everything for her. Anyways he had realized that Her prince was not a real prince because he was in fact just a beggar always making all so The fairy princess wouldn't leave him with the fear to find himself alone without being accompanied by her beauty giving him the pride and glory of looking like a powerful prince, and also that The fairy princess needed the attention of two man, who would fight for her, making her feel valued and desired.

He knew Her prince enjoyed knowing the Enchanter fighting for his princess who he owned. As the Enchanter was The prince of melodies he could go anywhere like the water because the kingdom of melodies was in the air everywhere.

CHAPTER 45
THE ENCHANTER FINDS OUT SOME PEOPLE GO STEAL IN HIS ROOM ON THE TWELVE FLOOR OF HIS ABONDONNED PALACE

The day after the Enchanter of the flute
went up to his abandoned building palace and
when arriving in his room on the dark, he
put his hand where he had hidden his plastic
string tool and nothing was there and put his
hand where he had hidden his gas spray to
cook his onions and was also gone, he walked
a few steps to the fire steel box and his chair
was also not there and looked around and
many things had been removed, one sleeping
bag was missing and one shoes of the pair
shoes he was planning to wear when coming
back was also gone. They had stolen his shoes
and many other tools. His writing paper notes
with all the poems and music pieces he wrote
for The fairy princess were all over the room,
somebody had been there and took his writing

plastic string tool and didn't respect his living place. He went down, but nobody had found the bag with The fairy princess's blue dress which he was keeping for many months, so he put inside that bag the other brown three flutes with the one other brown soprano so it was four plastic brown flutes of each size for the school he wanted to create, and also the five golden little bird flutes he bought for The fairy princess, and the new wooden flute she didn't want.

The day after his wheel tool attached to his wheel carrier had been knocked besides his abandoned building like if somebody tried to steal it, and was no longer able to ride, so he attached his wheel tool to the building steel gate, took his wheel carrier with one hand

and carried his music tools to go enchant, and when he arrived to his enchanting place, for the first time he stopped in the middle of the path with his mind was in the air or empty up in the clouds feeling totally lost. The fairy princess passed by. She didn't look at him totally ignoring him and disappeared walking to her living place. He was lost and she didn't feel he needed help but he sat and enchanted the streets. When he had finished enchanting he went to his building and saw his wheel tool had been knocked more times like with big stones and the locker couldn't open, they had knocked at the locker with stones and only could open it if breaking it.

The day after, when he came back from enchanting the street, again the wheel tool was totally gone, so he went to the capital take his other wheel tool he had brought from Innsbruck and went back to the town of The fairy princess with it. He also went to take back his tronic steel strings tool from The fairy princess's prince office which he would play in the streets to vary from his flute, and he hid it also in a new place as his magical drum and the big long bamboo tube to make low sounds to make music with the cricket's rhythm. They found again his two new places. He was back from the capital and his bamboo tube was gone, his tronic steel string tool and his black bag with the five golden bird flutes, the four brown plastic flutes, the new wooden flute and the baby blue dress for The fairy princess disappeared. In his room the fur he had bought, to make shoes was also missing. He realized somebody knew he was hiding in his abandoned building all his music tools and all the private belongings he owned. So he brought all the music tools he was hiding and what was left to a friend to keep all safe. He went up to his room and his knew chair had been taken for the second time, so he didn't buy any chairs anymore and he would sit on a box when practicing his two music pieces without words #The Tango of Prague# and, #The tango of Diane# in front of the fire. He could not write singing words anymore for her, his heart had given the last breath but he was practicing those two pieces because he had to make them capture in order to share them to all the people of the world.

CHAPTER 46
AND THE ENCHANTER WAS SINGING ALL THE MUSIC PIECES HE WROTE FOR THE FAIRY PRINCESS IN THE CAPITAL AND IN HER TOWN

For one whole month the Enchanter of the flute and The fairy princess didn't cross each other. The Enchanter was enchanting with his new flutes in the old part of her town and he was also going often enchant in the capital with plastic sandals he bought for a few coins in the town where he got stolen his fur shoes and where he found his new wheel tool. The fairy princess was traveling with Her prince.

He didn't feel happiness anymore in her kingdom after speaking to her the last time when she told him that she couldn't make melodies with her flutes. He knew it was her hidden code language to hurt his feelings because he had accused Her prince to not care for the heart melodies of princesses but more for the comfort of their physical body. He had discovered again how interesting and exciting it was to be moving from kingdom to kingdom like he used to before staying one year in her kingdom, like he experienced in his last trip. And one evening up in his room looking at the fire, he felt releasement in his heart and the invisible forces made him feel that he could renounce on The fairy princess, because she was not ready to change her life and leave with him to enchant the world.

He was going back and forth a few days in each one, to the capital, and to the town of The fairy princess enchanting proclaiming his defeat and his departure, asking for the address of every person he would talk with to invite them to gathering before leaving

He was then singing with detachment and releasement, all the music pieces he wrote for The fairy princess.

In the capital he made one friend, a metal dog who never moved and he played his elegant music tool for him and he enchanted also the steel string tool standing always on a bench besides a water rising like jets where he was dreaming to dance the romance with The fairy princess...

As he had been stolen his plastic string music tool, he had bought another one to be able to capture the music piece #The Tango of Prague# on which he didn't manage to dance on the roof of his abandoned palace with The fairy princess on his music piece so every princess in the world could dance on it. He was looking to see if he would find another plastic string tool that he would like more. In tamsta the same store where he found his little plastic 7 coin flute, he found a plastic string tool with The fairy princess's exact name written on it and reserved it.

CHAPTER 47
THE FAIRY PRINCESS APPEARED INFRONT OF THE PAINTING OF HIS BUILDING

Some days later, while he was organizing his departure, when he was sitting calmly in around his abandoned palace in front of the painting of the hurt child, The fairy princess passed by walking, she was wearing the same dark soft green pants as in the last talk they had and he was also wearing the same dark soft green tshirt of the same color. He called her by her name, and she heard him and walked to him right away and asked him "How are you doing?" But he did not say how he was doing, he was very tired and he had been damaged his finger in the capital by a strong guy attacking him and he had also been attacked during the night under his two crying trees in the park where he wrote her all the poems but he didn't tell her and just answered "I am leaving your kingdom soon". Looking at him she said "It's too worm for you in my kingdom" He replied "It is not there is other reasons" He remained silent and remembered what the pendulum had said and asked her "So you don't like my abandoned palace?" And she replied "It looks scary" So he asked for the third time and last time "Would you like to dance for my plastic string romance in the nicest places of my palace? There is beautiful places for art dance in the third floor" And she replied "No I would not like it, I like dancing in front of people or with a prince but not for your plastic strings heart sounds" when it started slightly raining...She started moving her wrists like trying to seduce him as the beginning of a romantic serenade, but her plastic box started ringing, it was Her prince asking her where she was, probably to tell her to come to him in the warm because it was slightly raining and it was not safe for her risking to get sick. The Enchanter then understood that it would always be like this and had the feeling he wouldn't regret at all to leave her kingdom anymore. He understood Her prince would always interrupt when he was speaking with her so he was fulfilled by his departure and was sure the best was to leave and all was clear in his mind. And she asked "I have to go, do you have anything else to tell me before I go?" He answered "If you let me the time to think...ah yes now I think I remember, so would you like to come play your harp at the new building of my rich friend?" And she answered "You are asking me if I want to come play my harp?" And he said "Yes, you told me you would think about it" She said right away "No, I would not like it," And he did not speak any more and remained silent. Then she said "If you have nothing more to say I will go" And he said "If you don't let me the time to know what to say, you think things come like this...actually it makes me think that I lost my bamboo flute which I need for capturing the sounds with it and I bought for you exactly the same, could I borough yours?" She accepted and gave him a meeting time "We meet here early at nine tomorrow after I finish running, and I come bring you the bamboo flute" He said "I don't have a clock to awake me up and I don't sleep in my palace anymore" So she said "Ok then tell me where you sleep at the moment and I will bring it after running" So that's how they agreed, he explained her where he was sleeping and he added "But awake me up when you come bring your flute" And she left.

In the morning when the Enchanter of the flute awoke he thought The fairy princess forgot him because she did not awake him up and he could not see the flute. When he was going to pack his wheel carrier, he saw one flute he had bought for her on his trailer but it was not the one he asked her for, so he went to the office of Her princess and gave it back to him with a letter for her, saying...

"Thank you for thinking of me but, this is not the one flute I asked you, if you wish to lend to me the one I need as you said you would, you can come this evening meet me" But, she didn't come. And he renounced on capturing the sounds of her bamboo flute..."

CHAPTER 48
THE ENCHANTER BRINGS THE PLASTIC STRING TOOL ADMIRA TO HER PRINCE

Then the Enchanter was preparing the last gift for The fairy princess before disappearing from her kingdom, he went finally to buy the plastic string tool with her name,

He also bought a beautiful white dress and put in a big plastic bag with the pink soft cover that was hanging on the tree on the entrance of his building palace garden where he would hide some tools of him during all winter long. In the white dress paper gift, he laid one golden flute he found the factorious music tool store in the capital and inside the old plastic bag of her plastic string tool, he put a red dried rose and his softest flute with wooden appearance inside her plastic string tool bag and hanged the baby blue color pen he had used to write her all the poems and mind thoughts. Then he went to Her prince's office and told him "This is your princess's string tool" Her prince as always trying to give the Enchanter some trouble opened the string tool bag without respect and saw it was not her blue steel string tool and said with an aggressive voice "This is not my princess's blue string tool!" So the Enchanter thought fast a way to make Her prince bring it to The fairy princess, that was all he wanted before leaving her kingdom and told him "It is now, because it is her birthday gift" So Her prince said "Ah, one more gift, nice alright" And the Enchanter of the flute shook his hand telling him looking straight away in his eyes "Thank you for everything" distracting his mind so he would bring the plastic string tool to the The fairy princess.

He was organizing his departure and his wheel carrier tool was almost broken and he was looking for a place to hide it but it broke before bringing it to the capital and had to carry it until a wheel machine stopped and helped him to carry it to the big power wheel machine. From the capital station he pushed it until he found a fast letter shop and sent a fast letter to a friend princess to come pick up his elegant music tool that was too heavy. And there he was approaching nice princesses who were passing by the street distracting himself waiting for his friend who was going to come pick his elegant silver tool, when he saw a delightful princess approaching hearing in his heart, #I will speak to that princess# He walked a few steps crossing the wheel machine road approaching her asking "Where are you going?" She answered "Enchanter I don't have time I have to go to take the wheel power machine..." And then he saw, it was The fairy princess and became embarrassed because he didn't see at first it was her and replied "Oh it's you..." Then she thanked him "Thank you for my new plastic string tool" And added "I have to go, I am late for my power wheel machine" and kept walking up.

The Enchanter was impressed and took his elegant silver tool that was in his wheel carrier and started blowing on it in the middle of the road killing the time waiting for his friend and realized after, there, was a wall in the corner with the number 11 and the letter à...

The Enchanter knew he had to leave her kingdom cause he had realized that it was possible that the fairy princess of his dreams had chosen to love somebody else than him, and did not want to keep the promise she made to him in the invisible forces before coming to the earth, even if it was in front of the big power of the higher forces.

He abandoned the wheel carrier in one abandoned strange place and when he was ready, he went back to her town and made a tag in the highest wall of his abandoned palace on the longest word of her language, the tag was this words #and here on this roof the anchanter of the flute wanted to dance with The fairy princes# Then he left her kingdom riding his wheel tool in the middle of the night.

Before arriving to the neighbor kingdom, he saw a skunk dead in front of the middle of the road. He took the skunk with his arms and brought him to the garden next to the road, where he laid him in front of flowers. He stared at the lake nearby and when his heart had breathed the peace, he kept riding his wheel tool.

CHAPTER 49
THE ANCHANTER OF FLUTE FOLLOWS HIS WAY WITH OUT THE FAIRY PRINCESS

The Enchanter was crossing many towns and many places. When his knees would hurt, he would afford a ticket with the coins he would earn blowing with his flute to pay the big power machines.

He arrived to a place where there was part of a castle left from old times...Right in front was a fountain and he was thinking to blow his flute there the day after. He saw a very cute princess walking and called her but she couldn't hear him, she had music on her ears, so he walked to her and they spoke together. She told him that she would like to meet him again so they agreed to meet at the fountain the day after.

In the morning, he was as planned at the fountain enchanting the people and the kids.

That princess went to him and gave him a drink. He had seen an old trumpet that he liked, in the antic market happening that day but he had earned half of the price so he couldn't buy it. As she was generous and nice, she went to check her saving coins and went to buy the trumpet for him. On the trumpet the words Welt klang were written, which meant sounds of the earth...His wheel was flat but it was a Sunday so the shops were closed. She brought him to a box hanging on a wall that would want coins to give out in exchange rubber wheels, in the way to that box, it started raining strongly, they stopped under the umbrella of a bar waiting that the rain would stop. Before separating, they both agreed to meet again after his trip.

Rolling his wheel tool, he arrived to his brother and went to pick a few books of the story ## the anchanter of the flute and the fairy princess ## and commenced a long trip crossing many lands until arriving to the capital where wheel machines going fast were making smoke. He was trying to find some where to make capture his music pieces but everyone was busy and demanded lots of coins for that. He met a young boy though who told him to go join his in his living place where he had a tool to capture sounds. Where that boy lived was close to the sea side where he had planned to pass to reach the strange land crossing the sea with a boat. When he arrived to see that boy, he was giving him excuses to not meet, so as the Enchanter was an action person who kept his goals in mind, he crossed the sea without his music pieces captured.

In the last town before reaching the sea, he fell very sick, some people on the streets had given him a plastic glass with soup that might have a bactery. He was very week and could not enchant with his flute. That night he went to sleep with one coin in his pocket and awoke up very hungry and very week, he had not enough coins to afford what he wanted to eat, so was asking the people in the shop if they had twenty cents of a coin so he could buy a small fish inside a tin. When he had the tin in his hands he noticed the price and he had not enough, so he put it back where he took it. He was asking to the people inside the food shop again if they had twenty cents cause the tin was one coin and twenty cents but they were ignoring him. In that kingdom all the people had become without sense and full of anger. So he decided to buy only cheap chips costing less than one coin. When he arrived in front of that woman to pay the cheap chips, he handed to her the only coin he had and the chips when not nicely she asked "And where is the tins you took from us?" He answered "Where it was" She told him with aggressing voice "Give us back what you stolen from us" He retorted "I have stolen nothing from you, the tin is in its place where I left it" An evil person who was supposed to be the security said with an aggressive voice "Show us the inside of your music tool!" But the Enchanter of the flute retorted "I have taken nothing from your shop and it's my music tool" That woman and that man started to insult him and pushing him violently towards the inside of the shop...The Enchanter of the flute was very week because he was very sick but focused on so they would not touch his string music tool with which he was practicing his singing music pieces and The tango of Prague, because he knew this two persons were completely evil. He asked to the young couple buying their foo to call the national guards but they were not heroes and did not help him. The Enchanter of the flute was telling them that the goodness of the invisible forces of the good god power were going show them how to behave...But they were repeating with mockery arrogance that they didn't believe in god, when a group of five strong workers came in to the shop. The Enchanter of the flute noticed one was a good person and asked him help. That person was small but brave and had an opened heart and helped him so he could go away eat his chips and rest without having to fight.

CHAPTER 50
THE ENCHANTER ARRIVES TO THE STRANGE KINGDOM WHERE WAS THE MOST FAMOUS LANGUAGE IN THE HISTORY MADE UP

He arrived to the harbor still quite sick but managed to go in to the boat, crossed the sea and arrived in to the kingdom where they made up the most famous language of all the times...

Besides the harbor, a beautiful white cliff was always still there. He was staring at it until he rode his wheel tool on the dark evening arriving after the sun fell sleep. He arrived to a crossroads where was written folkstone and followed and found himself on a long sloping road going down. Once in the town he followed down a small sloping street and then went up asking to stranger where he could find a food shop. He got indicated a direction he followed. He bought his tasty marmite, it was his favorite lunch and went to eat some with bread on a cliff in front of the sea side listening to the waves. After he had finished, he went down a rocky zigzag, he felt like in a rocky world. When he arrived to the water he laid his sleeping tools to rest and went to blow his new old trumpet for the sea on the rocks by the beach. When he had sent his inspiration to the vast water land he went to lay on his mattress. One person stopped in front of him speaking to his plastic box, so he told that person "Excuse me I would like to sleep?" That person told him "Hey you, don't you see I am talking to my plastic box don't talk to me or I punch you on the face" walking away. The Enchanter of the flute was worried so he packed off and went up the rocky zigzag and stopped on the cave, he tried the echo with his voice and imagined The fairy princess there playing her harp. He made a few more walks and stopped in the next cave farther up and took his favorite plastic flute the black crow, he blew with it while the waves were resonating all over the rocky zigzag. After he grabbed his plastic string tool and made sound a serenade but there was no body listening except the sea waves moving making water sounds and the still rocks amplifying the sounds of his serenade. After, he saw a rock where he wanted to sleep on, he imagined himself sleeping up there safe from violent plastic box victims and tried reach it, but it was slippery so didn't manage. Then he went up threw the rocky zigzag at top and met a nice gentleman who bought the first book called #the anchanter of the flute and the fairy princess# then he rode his wheel tool looking for a safe place to sleep away from the rain and met a couple who invited him to sleep at their living place and wanted to know his story so they bought another book. In the morning, while he was eating his marmite with bread, an officer informed him that it wasn't allowed to put a basket box on the floor in order to receive coins. There was already too many people doing that in their kingdom, so he hid the coin box and left his little violet carpet. When he had finished eating, he rode around the town and finally went to the zigzag where he enchanted with his flutes and received some coins from people walking by...

In the night he went to the cemetery to sleep on a grave. He hid himself with his violet cover that he attached to one grave and to the trumpet box. In the morning he was awoken by an old bold man moving his cane trying to scare him, he was repeating "You cannot sleep here" The Enchanter of the flute was retorting "God allowed me to" And the old bold man was repeating "You cannot sleep here, is not allowed" The Enchanter didn't have the intention to let him win, so he kept asking "How is possible that is not allowed if I slept here last night?" The bold man kept moving his cane, repeating "You cannot sleep here, is not allowed" moving his cave, until he knocked the Enchanter's trumpet box and made it fall. He seemed then satisfied and turned his back walking away calmly as if it was just a simple comedy.

The Enchanter of the flute packed laughing inside, he thought that man was one of the funniest old man he ever met. He went to buy more marmite and went to the zigzag enchant with his flute and got some more coins. Then he went down to the sea and met a young man who captured the sounds of the waves and the melodies if his black crow flute while he was walking on the stones besides the waves, he slipped on a wet stone and felt in to a wave. He took off his wet socks and walked up bare feet to the clock of the zigzag, and met a little girl called Zodede who he enchanted with his flute. She moved like dancing for his sounding melody. He also danced blowing his flute to amuse her and she liked it so when he stopped because his heart was tired, she repeated "I want you to dance again" So he danced again every time she asked him to. The Enchanter of the flute offered to her his book but she did not want it and said again "I want you to dance again" so he danced once again for her blowing his flute at the same time and after with his harmonica. Her grandpas was taking her back home and the Enchanter of the flute gave her his music code to bring with her but she said "I don't want it" and repeated "I want you to dance again" so he danced again blowing his flute until her grandfather finally took Zodede by her hand to bring her home.

In the night he slept close to there under the bandstand in front of the clock and awoke with a marvelous sun rising on the horizon. Many people were running. He tried to stop them so they could capture the beauty of the sun rise but nobody listened and kept running. His clothes were starting to smell so he went to the sea side danced on his clothes cleaning them moving them with his feet on the sand with the salty water when light rain started falling so he could also clean his hair. When the rain stopped, he put on the totally wet clothes so they would dry with the wind when riding his wheel tool.

He saw the officer again who asked him how he was doing. The Enchanter of the flute explained him that he went to the sea side clean his clothes with salty sand. The officer was astonished and asked him if the salt was clean. The Enchanter explained him that the salt was natural and efficient to clean the clothes with. The officer wanted to help him giving him an address where cleaning clothes machines, and food was a free social help but the Enchanter told him his priority was to create moving drawings so all the kids could watch his story and listen to his music pieces at the same time. The officer was impressed, he asked him if he could be part of his story explaining him that he made himself stories with drawings so they became friends.

After, the Enchanter of the flute went to blow his flute for the kids in the zigzag rocks and then slept under the bandstand again. He awoke again with an amazing sun rising as beautiful as the previous morning. Again there was people running and he was trying to stop them again to show them the amazing sun rising but nobody listened. He realized the people there had different purposes so he left to look for the Stone Land.

CHAPTER 51
THE ENCHANTER GOES LOOK FOR THE STONE LAND

He was crossing many fields and lands and arrived to the capital of that, huge island but there everyone was busy with their plastic boxes so he didn't stay long and left to the Stone Land looking for peace. He was rolling his wheel tool, when a quite small person was passing with his small boat by small canal besides the road calling him "Hey!" out loud wanting to speak with him. When they were closer he told the Enchanter that he will let him live in a boat he had in the capital and would give it to him, so the Enchanter put his wheel tool in the boat and was driven back to the capital on the small boat with that person. When they arrived at the capital after all night driving the boat, the Enchanter of the flute felt very tired.

He did not feel all right around that person who was always shouting complaining about what people in his life had done to him, so he renounced on that boat to stay in peace and kept his initial destination with his heart a little oppressed after that experience. The Enchanter of the flute was writing his book story in libraries. With his soul still a little damaged by the boat person he entered in a nice rustic library after trying to enjoy the day and saw a marvelous little girl, called Saffron, and blew melodies to her. When he had finished, Saffron came close to him with and told him "You are lovely" There, very close were her parents, they were pleased that the Enchanter had blown his melodies in to Saffron and thanked him.

The Enchanter's brakes had broken so he was pushing his wheel tool on stiff paths down and up, down because he couldn't stop and up because the paths were too stiff and his wheel tool too heavy. On the stiffest path he ever was, he found at the top a group of cows to who he blew on his favorite black crow flute. All the cows were enchanted and were slowly approaching him. The rain started falling so he kept rolling his wheel tool fast down and crossed many other fields, rivers and pushed downs and up his wheel tool so many times without brakes until he arrived to a town where he stayed some time, and could repair his brakes. There were lots of people sleeping outside. Some of them were telling him that he had to move and could not enchant there with his flute, they were pretending it was their place and their town, but as usual the Enchanter proved them he was strong and showed them nobody could own the streets...

CHAPTER 52
THE 50 BOOKS OF HIS STORY BRING HIM LUCK

After a few weeks in that town he met a young lady who agreed to receive his books and when she had received them she gave him a meeting by a fast letter. He was there while it was raining waiting for her for one hour with wet shoes but she did not come.

The day after he read her letter saying "Sorry but my mother had a problem and I decided that was way more important than you" That day he had lost his violet cover in the nature. He was rolling his wheel tool along the river when he saw hundreds of crows flying all at the same time making an enormous black wave in the sunset sky when almost there was no light. Then he rode farther his wheel tool and found animals in the dark but he couldn't see how they looked them. He could only see white moving and guessed it was sheep. He blew on his black crow flute for them and then he went to sleep inside an enormous big plastic tent close to a restaurant he had seen earlier where he slept calmly protected from the wind blowing all night long.

The day after he went to see those white animals again who were in fact white sheep as he had thought. He blew his black crow for the sheep and then he went to the second meeting with that young woman to take his books. This time she came at the exact time she had told him to come. He had then the fifty books of his story with The fairy princess that he placed in the front of his wheel tool. Feeling ready to leave to the next destination. He jumped with his wheel tool in to the big power machine, he had not enough energy to ride his wheel tool and was almost sick. He had lost his violet cover so he was cold at night but he had not enough coins to buy another one. As he was always attacked by homeless in the last town he was, he couldn't earn much coins.

CHAPTER 53
THE ENCHANTER SICK ALMOST DIES

He crossed many towns totally sick and week and arrived to a small town and in a library a pretty princess cold Estella bought a book of his right away, it was the third and then had eleven coins, it was half of the price for a new violet cover. When he arrived to the next town he met a princess who told him she would buy one book, but she did not come to the meeting she had given him. That night, sick as he had never been, he felt almost dying. In the morning when he awoke, he could barely move for a while, so he forced himself to stand up and packed his sleeping tools to look for a safer place. He arrived to a prayer house where he laid almost feeling dead, when a gentle prince noticed he was sick laying not so far from the door so he went to his living place bring him potatoes soup. He also bought another book of his story, so then the Enchanter had twenty two coins and went to buy right away a new soft cover of the color beige because there was no violet. Eating lots of spicy hot food, he healed slowly after five days.

By the main street of the town, there was a big porch besides a big tall clock where was a very good echo to make resonate his flute but always there was a person living on the street talking with a plastic box and smoking. The Enchanter of the flute was annoyed by his talks and his smokes but found another nice place where to enchant. He was there in evenings enchanting all the kids passing by. In front was a garbage bin where around came many rats showing up when not body was walking the street. The rats allowed the Enchanter to blow his flute in their territory, he made melodies and the rats could hear. He was giving them most of the food he was receiving food instead of coins, the rats were happy with him. Many people were handing to him paper coins of ten or twenty worth coins, so he was giving them books of his story in exchange of their generosity.

One evening two little sister princess came to him with each one, one paper coin of ten coins worth and he asked them each one their turn the same thing "Do you like reading?" and to her sister "Do you like reading?" and they answered yes both of them each one their turn too, so he gave to each one, one book.

In that town, he had managed to earn fast many coins in, it was almost enough to make capture his singing music pieces by an expert but he didn't know by who yet. He passed by a town where he bought a tent for a cheap price but in that town the guards came to tell him that he needed to apply for the license if he wanted to enchant so he went to the council but there, he was told that he needed a living address in order to blow his flute so he left.

When he was rolling his wheel tool the rain was falling so he stopped in a porch until it stopped raining and he rode again but again it started raining but he kept riding feeling the emotion of discovery. He kept riding until he saw a prayer house where besides a little porch. He thought he could sleep there the night safe from the rain. When he got closer, he saw the door was opened, and entered his sleeping bags and his wheel tool. He went to pray to the highest above what he needed, receiving the peace in his heart and then explored the place. There was a piano so he hit with his finger to make sound melodies. After, in silence still he remained some time, when he heard in his mind "You will sleep here" He placed his mattress and his sleeping bags. He wanted to read his music pieces' poems to practice them so he went to search for matches. He knocked at the door of the first living place he saw where he asked for matches and as he asked he received what he needed. Behind the man who brought him the matches was a little boy drinking from a milk baby bottle. He enchanted the little boy talking with his soft voice and went back to the prayer house. From the cemetery, he saw light inside. When he got in, he saw a man dressed like a priest, he introduced himself handing to him his two hands "My name is Nick Himt" He asked "Are you on a journey or you are a traveling on the streets?" and the Enchanter of the flute asked on his turn "What means in a journey and what means traveling on the streets?" Nick replied "Well journey means a travel on the streets t and the other means you don't have anywhere to stay" So he explained him "Well my situation is both at the same time" So Nick said "Well as Jesus would do, as you are not an alcoholic and you seem very nice person and I was going to close that is why I am here but I won't close because you are here so you will close yourself in, is there something I may do for you?" The Enchanter answered "As I just have two slices of bread for my marmite and my butter and it is a poor dinner, I would need more bread" So Nick said "I will come back in a few minutes if you wait for me" The Enchanter of the flute sat in his camping set and after a few minutes Nick opened the door again and handed to him two more slices of bread, little cheddar crisps and an apple, and he left saying "I let you in the peace of god"

The Enchanter spread his marmite butter toast, ate the crisps, sang one song and fell sleep. While he was stretching his two arms behind his head in the morning, Nick opened the door and said "I came to see if you are all right, have a safe journey" and left. So the Enchanter packed everything and kept rolling his wheel tool.

He rode more and more and arrived to a field where sheep were but bigger and with more hair than usual. He blew on his black crow flute for them. They were listening to his melody with emotion. He realized that animals were more sensitive than humans. He thought he had a path with sheep because he felt love for them and had the vision of living with them and decided then to live in high lands with sheep in a small house heated with fire...

In the next town, he met a nice fairy with orange hair she was very pretty and little small, she was lost in life. She wished to have somebody with who she could share her life but she didn't find anyone with who she could live in the nature as she was dreaming. The Enchanter liked her so he offered her to live with him in the high land forest, in a little living place where they could heat with fire feeding them self with mushroom soaps living like a real wizard and a real fairy together in the peace of the nature and with sheep. At first she seemed enchanted by him and the Enchanter felt so calmly secured in her living place but after her plastic box rang and she talked to a man who liked to sniff a ketam-powder and instead of staying with the Enchanter, she chose to go with that man and told the Enchanter "I am sorry I have to kick you out I am starting to not trust on you" The Enchanter was very disappointed but he understood that, that little fairy was really lost and also not ready for him as was The fairy princess, so he rode more thousands walks and slept besides another prayer house when in the morning a gentle awoke him handing to him some warm drink and giving him ten coins in paper worth. It was the vicar of the prayer house. They were have a talk when suddenly a little bird landed on his wheel tool handle bar and the vicar exclaimed

"I have never seen this, it never happen to me before, this is a sign from the sky..."

CHAPTER 54
THE ENCHANTER' MUSIC PIECE THE TANGO OF PRAGUE FINALLY GETS CAPTURES

When he arrived to enchanter bury town
he found many new flutes in a shop and he
became happy, and was enchanting every day
and every evening receiving coins to pay his
news flutes. The princess Delphi Blue was
keeping the coins he was earning because so
many coins were heavy to carry and she had
the power to send coins to people. When he
found out Sekunda could capture his music
pieces, he asked to the princess Delphi Blue
to send all the coins she was keeping for him
to Sekunda, After he left to find the place
He was crossing towns and lands enchanting
receiving coins. He was in a dangerous town
called York where there was lots of crappy
people sleeping on the streets who were not
kind and were ready to hurt him to get his

coins. One of them threatened him saying that he had to go blow his flute somewhere else or he was going to bring his friends to beat him up. Young princesses were putting their saving coins in the Enchanter's basket coin telling him "You are lovely" while the neighbor crappy homeless was waiting for the little princesses to go so he could attack the Enchanter with his friends and a dog. They did not want to work and were jalousie of the Enchanter's success. There he had earned enough coins to give to Sekunda for all his music pieces captured.

He finally arrived to Sekunda the chosen one who was going to capture The tango of Prague.

When he was tuning his strings, before singing his music pieces in front of Sekunda, and one plastic string broke. He had to run rolling his wheel tool to buy a new string. When he was back he sang all his music pieces playing his plastic string tool and Sekunda captured all the sounds but there was one missing, it was The Tango of Prague and Sekunda said "I don't have time, we report this music piece to next time" Going down the hill rolling fast, his two wheels going back to center his plastic string tool fell from the front and broke in two pieces scratched by his front wheel on the street floor.

He was then worried, but he had met a princess whose father was a music string tool repairer but she was not in town and she didn't want to help him, so he went to buy a special glue and glued the neck broke in two pieces again in one piece and could practice The Tango of Prague.

When he Sekunda had sat the next sound capturing moment, the Enchanter of the flute went to the meeting and Sekunda captured finally The tango of Prague. The Enchanter of the flute then had accomplished his goal and could leave that strange land satisfied.

All released he went to his brother again, when an invisible war started. Everyone was afraid of an enemy who was called crown and who could be anyone but nobody knew if the enemy was them self's or the other ones right in front. Many people of them were wearing masks because they were suspecting a little creature could kill them without them having seeing it in real. All the boarders of all the kingdoms were closed because of that creature as tiny as invisible, but as the Enchanter was brave and always did what was not allowed, he crossed again the continent rolling his wheel tool riding thousands of distances and arrived to one of the highest land on earth searching for the little house he was given years ago because he felt like he needed to rest in the nature.

When he arrived after so many days rolling his wheel tool, the woman who had told him he could have her small house was there inside sleeping. She was living there alone and she had changed. She seemed to be totally traumatized. He did not have time to take care of witches with grey ideas and grey visions, he had to Enchant all the kids of all the world with his plastic flute and his music pieces, so he went to that kingdom's capital when he was contacted by the invisible prince Barbers because his community wanted to spread the book he had written about the story with The fairy princess to all the people of all the kingdoms of the world so everyone could read the story he had with The fairy princess and could hear The Tango of Prague and all the music pieces he wrote for her...

END OF THE STORY

I understand I must
Accept her fear
Today I met a real Poppy
And it made me so happy

She asked how to trust
Explain for me she is dear
This instants on the rain
Yes… life is insane

I crossed her soft wave
My feelings I write because I am brave
Love is strange
It appears like a revenge

If you fly away
To miss you I may
Besides you
Or in front of you

You inspire my heart
You are to blame for this art
I wouldn't let you go
But for you it has to be slow

In the encounter of today
On your hands my love I want to lay
Like a beginner in life I feel
I will wait like a deal

There is no protection when it appears there
Special feel that life makes me dare
Don't let your self be scared
The love to you was offered

If you follow what the peace gives
Then your heart the love receives
Like a puzzle my words are encrypted
If you understand them your fear then is
defeated

Ridiculous it is
My thoughts here I release
When you hear a child give you his love
You take it as soft as a glove

When another by you is tendered
Will you have his soul heard
If his mind is true
As with words your being he tried to drew

Would you let him alone
As talking from each bone
He sees you walk away
As if with you was his way

All this emotions in my mind
I don't' live like a blind
If everything could be eternal
To go with you would be natural

So I told you...I let you go
So life you again to me back will blow
Always regrets can appear
But time makes everything clear

I let my mind in peace
Tomorrow this words to you I will release

I have seen your need for love
Cause you know of all that is above
That is of mine a famous rime
No pride on it to clime

But my inside is moved
Sort of feeling loved
Or to be like lost
Of all is the most

How to explain or to classify
If it is the only one that you defy
When you cross you shall recognise
And have to realise

In be twin all this horrible
Good is still possible
I am like a child

And you are to me the life that smiled

Lightning Source UK Ltd.
Milton Keynes UK
UKHW010654081220
374827UK00001B/7